# CHASING PARADISE

A PREQUEL TO THE *STANDING IN HOLY PLACES* SERIES

# CHASING PARADISE

A PREQUEL TO THE *STANDING IN HOLY PLACES* SERIES

## BY CHAD DAYBELL

spring creek
BOOK COMPANY
Rexburg, Idaho

ISBN: 978-1-944657-10-9
e. 1

Published by:
Spring Creek Book Company
P.O. Box 1013
Rexburg, Idaho 83440

www.springcreekbooks.com

Cover design © Spring Creek Book Company

Printed in the United States of America
Printed on acid-free paper

# AUTHOR'S NOTE

⁓

This is a work of fiction, but it is based on true experiences. The descriptions of the Spirit World, and even the actions of various spirits, are based on actual accounts of those who have had near-death experiences. Each near-death experience is unique—some people found themselves in Paradise when they crossed over, while others arrived in Spirit Prison—but a general thread of truth runs through them all. I based the book on experiences found in many publications, but I found the following books to be most helpful in giving a portrayal of the Spirit World:

Life Everlasting by Duane Crowther
I Saw Heaven by Lawrence Tooley
Return from Tomorrow by George Ritchie
Spirit World Manifestations by Joseph Heinerman

These books all share basic truths regarding the Spirit World. They make it clear that the Spirit World is here on earth, but in a different dimension. Another truth is that spirits can touch each other, spirit to spirit. Righteous spirits like to hug, and wicked ones like to fight. You'll see both cases in this book.

I also relied heavily on the teachings found in the Standard Works of the LDS Church, particularly President Joseph F. Smith's vision of the Spirit World found in Doctrine & Covenants Section 138.

Finally, this book would not have been written without a

personal experience that showed me how close the Spirit World truly is. When I attended BYU, I took a Family History class and helped complete the temple work for several families on my wife Tammy's ancestral line. We felt confident these ancestors had accepted the work and were progressing in the Spirit World.

Then in 2001 I felt a nagging feeling that someone had been forgotten during our previous genealogical work. Through a series of little miracles, we discovered a young woman named Rachel had indeed been overlooked during our earlier family history work. Several years had passed since the temple work had been done for her parents and siblings, and I received the impression she was very anxious to join her family.

We submitted Rachel's name for temple work, and Tammy's brother went to the Provo Temple with his daughter to complete Rachel's work. During the baptism and the confirmation, both of them could feel Rachel's presence. Later in the week, Tammy completed Rachel's endowment work, and then Rachel was sealed to her parents.

The unusual part came two days later when Rachel, in spirit form, visited Tammy's Grandma Cooper, who wasn't aware we were doing Rachel's temple work. Rachel shared with Grandma Cooper how grateful she was her work had been completed and that she was now be reunited with her parents and siblings.

With that in mind, I dedicate this book to Rachel for patiently waiting all those years to join her family in Paradise.

Now on with the story.

# AN IMPORTANT MESSAGE

You are holding a unique book. I should know, since I'm the one who found the original manuscript. My name is Guy Calvert, and I'm still surprised and humbled I was chosen to be the book's recipient. I rarely read anything besides the newspaper, but this story really grabbed my attention.

I found it in my office—a small room in an old brick building in Provo, Utah. I build duplexes for a living, so there are usually stacks of architectural plans and contracts covering my desk. But I immediately spotted this manuscript when I unlocked my office that bright October morning. The white, carefully stacked pages were sitting in the center of my chair in stark contrast to the scattered papers on my desk.

I was a little spooked at first, since no one else has a key to my office, but I cautiously picked up the pile of handwritten pages. The strange circumstances of its appearance caused me to immediately start reading it. It was a fascinating story about a girl named Tina Marlar and her family. Before I knew it, I was nearly halfway through the manuscript.

I glanced at the clock and was stunned to see two hours had passed. I had an important meeting with a painting contractor at noon, but I flipped through the remaining pages and saw I could probably finish the book before then. At 11:30 I read the final page and my heart was racing.

I carefully restacked the manuscript and hurried home to show it to my wife Flora. She was washing dishes and was surprised to see me. "What about your meeting?" she asked.

I smiled nervously. "I'll still make it to my meeting, but could you read this manuscript this afternoon?"

She looked at me strangely. "Is it a contract?" she asked.

"No, it's a story I found in my office. I'll explain later."

When I returned home that night, Flora met me at the door. She said, "We have to get this published as soon as possible."

I agreed, and we searched through the Yellow Pages for a publisher. The nearest publisher required manuscripts to be printed, so Flora spent the next two days typing the story on our computer without changing a word. We printed it off and drove to the company's offices. The editor-in-chief wasn't in, so we left the manuscript and a short note with the secretary.

After an anxious few days, I received a call back from the editor. He said he liked the story a lot, but he was concerned that our note had referred to the manuscript as a "true story." I explained the circumstances of how the manuscript was found, and he invited us to meet with the publisher and himself later that afternoon.

Our meeting went smoothly, and both men treated us very kindly. I never did convince them the story was true, but in the end they did offer us a contract—with an agreement the manuscript would be published as a novel. I told them that would be fine, as long as I could tell my side of the story in this introduction.

Despite what others might think, I sincerely believe this book tells the story of Tina Marlar. I'm beginning to get an inkling as to why I was given the manuscript. The experience has already changed my life, and I feel it will continue to do so. After years of procrastination, Flora and I have decided to serve a mission for the LDS Church. We sent our papers in last week. We don't know where we're going yet, but as you'll see, I'll bet we spend some time in Kansas!

Sincerely,

Guy Calvert
Provo, Utah

# CHAPTER ONE

The elegant two-story building again caught Tina Marlar's eye as she and her older sister Kim walked past it for the third time. Crowds of people were eagerly going inside, but Tina had no desire to get spooked.

"Come on, Tina," Kim said. "You're fifteen years old! How can you come to Disneyland and not go into the Haunted Mansion?"

Tina shrugged. "You know how I feel. I get scared even watching Halloween cartoons. I'm sure that ride will give me nightmares."

"That's fine," Kim said with a smile, tugging her sister toward the mansion. "Dad will need someone to keep him awake tonight when we drive to Las Vegas."

Tina was still hesitant, but she noticed the people coming out of the mansion's exit seemed to be fine. Some were even smiling. "Oh, all right," she said.

Kim laughed happily and guided Tina toward the mansion. They hurried through the gate and after a brief wait in line, a Disney employee motioned them through the front door. The girls found themselves crammed into a small lobby with fifty other people.

"Um, I've changed my mind," Tina whispered, grabbing Kim's arm, but the door shut behind them and a deep, frightening voice welcomed them into the mansion. Tina suddenly found it hard to breathe as the floor seemed to drop and previously innocent paintings on the walls stretched into ghoulish images. A door finally opened, and they walked down a darkened hall before climbing into a two-seated black buggy for a ride through the mansion. Tina clung to her sister's arm, and Kim shook her loose.

"You realize this is all fake, don't you?" Kim asked, slightly annoyed. "This isn't any more real than Toontown. Now sit back and enjoy it!"

Tina felt herself relax a little, and she was actually impressed by the images of ghosts dancing around a large dinner table. "How do they do that?" she asked, looking for a video projector.

She even smiled a little as they passed through a cemetery with several ghosts sitting around singing songs and making jokes. There was even a ghost dog howling along. Tina was startled, though, toward the end of the ride. The buggy turned to face a mirror, and astonishingly, a cartoonish, smiling ghost appeared in the mirror between the two sisters.

"Let's take him home with us!" Kim said with a laugh, but then the image faded away and the girls hopped out of the buggy. As they walked out of the exit, Kim put her arm around her sister's shoulder.

"See, that ride wasn't so terrible," Kim said. "Let's go again!"

Tina merely shook her head and took a seat on a nearby bench.

"What's wrong?" Kim asked.

Tina looked up at her. "Do you really think there are spirits all around us?"

"I don't think so," Kim said with a smile. "Did it frighten you that badly?"

"A little," Tina said. "I'll be fine, but if that ride is anything like what happens to us when we die, I want to live forever."

Kim checked her watch and said, "Oops, we don't have time anyway. Mom and Dad will be waiting for us. Let's go."

The girls had promised to meet their parents a half-hour before closing time in front of Sleeping Beauty's Castle. Kim led the way through the crowds and was the first to see their parents, who were the only adults in sight wearing Mickey Mouse ears.

"You two are strange," Kim said as the girls reached them. "Aren't you embarrassed to be wearing those hats?"

Their father Frank grinned. "Not at all. We've been saving them for you."

He placed his set of ears on Tina's head, and their mother Carmen slipped hers onto Kim. The girls protested and ripped them off, but then they noticed the hurt look on Frank's face.

"Dad, don't give us that frown," Tina said, but his expression didn't change. The girls slowly put the ears back on, slid their arms around each other and smiled so Carmen could take their photo. As the camera flashed, Frank instantly grinned again.

"Great!" he said. "That's a picture I'll always cherish."

An older couple had been watching the exchange. The man pointed at Frank's jacket, which bore a colorful Hill Air Force Base insignia.

"Are you from Utah?" the man asked.

"Yep," Frank said. "We moved to Layton a few weeks ago."

"How about that," the woman said. "We're from Brigham City. Do you happen to know Bill and Janet Francom? They used to be in our ward."

"Ward?" Frank asked as his smile faded a little.

"Sorry," the man said. "I guess you're not LDS."

"Nope. I know a lot of Mormons, though."

"Well, have fun," the woman said, smiling at the girls in their Mickey Mouse ears. "Maybe we'll see you around sometime."

As the couple walked away, Tina took her father by the arm. "I didn't know you knew a lot of Mormons," she said.

Frank shrugged. "In the Air Force, you meet all kinds of people."

Kim interrupted by saying, "We just went through the Haunted Mansion, and I want to go again before closing time. I know Tina doesn't want to go, but how about one of you?"

Frank wasn't too fond of the Haunted Mansion either, so he nudged his wife. "Why don't you go with Kim? I wanted to go on Splash Mountain one more time, and I'm sure Tina will go with me, right?"

Tina gave a relieved smile. "I'll take a rabbit singing 'Zip-a-dee-do-dah' over those ghosts anytime."

❧

After Frank and Tina had boarded one of Splash Mountain's plastic logs and started floating through the ride, Frank had a few moments to reflect on what a good experience this trip to California had been for his family.

Frank had been in the Air Force since he was a teenager. He'd seen most of the world—and all it had to offer—by the time he was 24. He had been on the path to self-destruction until that day nearly twenty years ago when he'd met Carmen, a beautiful girl from Peru who had just arrived in the United States. She had calmed him down and had been a great mother to the girls, especially during his frequent tours of duty.

This vacation made Frank realize how much of his daughters' lives he had missed over the years. Kim had turned 17 in February and would graduate from high school in less than a year. She'd certainly gotten his genes, with her light brown hair and pale skin. This was in sharp contrast to her younger sister.

Tina was 15, and her mother's striking Peruvian features were becoming evident. Frank was aware Tina's dark hair, flashing eyes and olive skin were attractive to the boys. Thankfully Tina hadn't shown any interest in return, but Frank realized his daughters would be grown up and gone before he knew it.

Frank snapped back to reality as the plastic log dropped over the edge of Splash Mountain and plummeted through the mist. All nostalgic thoughts were forgotten as he and Tina happily screamed their lungs out!

❧

As the hours of driving back home dragged on, Frank wished they'd just stayed in a hotel in Los Angeles after their long Saturday at Disneyland. He had to be back to work on Monday, though, and none of them had wanted to drive 13 hours on Sunday.

They finally rolled into Las Vegas at 2 a.m on Sunday morning, and Frank found a cheap hotel with a vacancy. Carmen and the girls basically sleepwalked into the room, and it was past 9 a.m. before they all woke up.

Frank was frustrated they had overslept despite facing another long drive to reach northern Utah that evening, and he herded the family into the car.

"We'll eat somewhere along the way," he told them.

Soon the Luxor Pyramid loomed on the right side of the freeway, and Kim begged Frank to take a drive down the Las Vegas Strip. He hadn't seen the Strip himself in more than two decades and wouldn't mind seeing the newest buildings.

"Oh, why not," Frank told her. "Let's take a look."

It actually turned out to be good timing. The sidewalks were empty, and only a few other cars were on the street.

"Where is everybody?" Tina asked.

"Asleep," Frank said. "When we pulled into town last night, this place was still hopping. I guess Sunday morning is when everyone recovers from all of their partying."

Carmen pointed to a casino that was advertising a cheap breakfast buffet, and they decided to fill up on food before hitting the freeway again. When they piled out of the car, Frank found a silver dollar on the pavement.

"It must be my lucky day," he said. He spotted a row of slot machines just inside the casino. "I gave up gambling years ago, but how about if we divide any winnings?"

The girls enthusiastically agreed, and Frank slipped the silver dollar into one of the machines. He pulled the arm back, and they watched the wheels lock into place, followed by the clink of coins hitting the tray.

"Hey, not bad," Frank said, scooping up five silver dollars.

Tina pleaded for him to try again, but Frank just smiled and handed a silver dollar to each of them. "Here you go," he said. "Now you can tell people something that I surely can't say—you've been a winner every time you've gambled."

Tina smiled at his suggestion. "You're right, Dad," she said. "I'm going to keep this silver dollar for as long as I live."

A short time later they drove out of Las Vegas and back onto I-15 heading toward Utah. They were admittedly feeling a bit overwhelmed by the sights of the city.

"I don't know if I would want to live there," Kim said, "but I guess it's the only place you can see an Egyptian pyramid, the Statue of Liberty, and the Eiffel Tower within a few blocks of each other. How convenient!"

By late afternoon they reached central Utah, and everyone had dozed off except Frank. As they approached the city of Nephi he exited the freeway and drove slowly down Main Street. Tina awakened in the back seat, and she looked into the rearview mirror at her father. He had a weird look in his eyes, but she figured it was from the long hours he'd been driving.

Tina was curious but stayed silent as Frank turned onto a side street and parked in front of a small white house. He studied it carefully. A woman was working in the garden along the side of the house, and she glanced at the car. Frank suddenly hit the gas and turned the car around, returning to Main Street and heading back to the freeway.

"What was all that about?" Tina asked.

Her voice made Frank jump. "What are you doing awake?" he asked with a hint of anger.

"I woke up when you pulled off the freeway," Tina said. "Did you know that lady?"

"I used to know the family that lived there," Frank said. "I think that woman was one of the daughters."

"You've actually been to Nephi before? I never knew that."

"I guess it never came up," Frank said.

"Well, let's go back and say hello," Tina said. "Did Mom know them? Maybe she'd like to meet them. It wouldn't hurt to stretch our legs."

Frank stared at her in the rearview mirror. "Just go back to sleep," he said. "Maybe that wasn't her after all."

# CHAPTER TWO

As soon as the car was unpacked, Kim immediately grabbed the phone to call her friend Nicole Nielsen. The two had several classes together and had become good friends in the few weeks Kim had attended Layton High School. After a brief phone conversation, Kim rushed into the laundry room where Carmen was emptying the suitcases of dirty clothes.

"Is it all right if I go over to Nicole's house?" Kim asked. "She wants to hear about the trip, plus she picked up some homework for me that I need to work on. I'll be back for dinner."

"That's fine," Carmen said. "Hey, why don't you invite her over? Dad's just going to order some pizza. I'd like to get to know Nicole a little better."

"I'll see if she can come," Kim said. "See you later!"

Carmen was pleased Kim had found a good friend so quickly. With all their moving around over the years, neither Kim nor Tina had made many lasting friends. The girls always had the lurking feeling they'd be moving within a few months, so why bother creating friendships? Carmen's heart had often ached for her daughters.

So Kim's blossoming friendship with Nicole was a pleasant surprise, and the older girls often included Tina on their outings to the Layton Hills Mall or to the movies. From all indications, Nicole was like most other Utah teenagers they had met—friendly and well-mannered. Carmen guessed Nicole was a Mormon, which was fine. Over the years, the girls had known kids from all religions, and it had made them tolerant and well-rounded.

When she and Frank were first married, Carmen had tried to follow her religion. She been raised as a Catholic in Peru and had attended Mass with her family on the major holidays, but without Frank's support, she had let her religious traditions fade away. She had some regrets about that, but she couldn't really blame Frank. Although he had never shown any interest in religion, he was a good husband and father who showed his daughters by example how to be a good citizen. She did note, however, that since moving to Utah, he'd been overly sensitive about the Mormons.

Kim arrived home and joined the family at the dinner table. The pizzas had just been delivered, and the others were digging in. "Nicole couldn't come over tonight," Kim said. "All of her married brothers and sisters showed up, and she felt she better stay home. I guess they all get together every Sunday evening."

"Typical Mormon behavior," Frank said under his breath before biting into another piece of pizza. Carmen and the girls looked at each other, wondering if they had heard him correctly.

"Dad, what did you say?" Kim asked. Tina noticed her father had that same strange look in his eyes that she'd seen during their stop in Nephi.

Frank sat up straight. "Oh, nothing. Mormons just put their families first. You ought to get used to that if you are going to be her friend."

His comments caught Kim off-guard. "How did you even know she was Mormon?" she asked. "I've never even mentioned it."

"I'm not blind," Frank said. "The last time she was here she was flashing that CTR ring to everyone."

Carmen slapped the table, causing their plates to jump. "Frank, would you be nice? I didn't even notice her ring! What's a CTR ring anyway?"

Frank looked at her. "CTR stands for 'Choose the Right.' The Mormons think if you wear that ring, you'll always do the right thing, but don't believe it for a minute! Carmen, if you want your girls to become misguided Mormons, then let them keep hanging out with Nicole." He looked over at Kim. "Has she ever mentioned the Book of Mormon to you?"

Kim hesitantly nodded. "Well, yes. She takes one to a class called Seminary right after our lunch break."

"Has she offered to let you read the book?" he asked, his voice rising.

Again Kim nodded.

Frank rubbed his face, started to say something, then let out a long breath. After a moment, he touched Kim's arm. "I'm sorry," he said. "It has been a long day."

He abruptly went out of the front door and slammed it behind him, leaving his family sitting in shock. Carmen reached out and took her daughters' hands.

"Everything will be okay," she said. "Your father is a wonderful man, except when it comes to the Mormons."

She paused and gave a sad smile. "I just remembered an incident that happened when we were first married. Your dad got into an ugly shouting match with a couple of Mormon missionaries that tried to talk to us, and maybe he's judging this whole state based on that argument, but that isn't fair. I knew several Mormons as a young girl in Peru, and they seemed like nice people."

Kim let out a sob, still shaken by her father's words. "Nicole's parents are nice people, and she's the best friend I've ever had."

Carmen could feel the pain Frank was causing within their family. "I know Nicole is a wonderful person, but until we sort this out with your father, maybe she shouldn't come over for a while. Just arrange to go to her house or meet at the mall, okay?"

Kim nodded, then climbed the stairs to her room. Tina sat silently, thinking about her father's actions in Nephi. She nearly told her mother about it, but then decided not to stir up any more trouble.

In the following days, Kim spent a lot of time with Nicole at school, but Nicole's name was never mentioned at home. Meanwhile, after Frank's angry comments, Tina hesitated to search out new friends since most of the kids were Mormons. In fact, she found herself rarely talking to anyone. The more she withdrew into herself, the less people seemed to bother her.

She hadn't been sleeping well, anyway. It all seemed tied to that trip through Disneyland's Haunted Mansion. The ride itself wasn't the problem—she now realized it really wasn't very spooky. But the whole experience had made her think about death.

"Is that all I have to look forward to?" she asked herself. "Will I spend eternity singing in graveyards and dancing around with other ghosts?"

The whole idea of death left her feeling hollow inside, especially after a dream she had shortly after their California trip. At least she hoped it had been a dream. Just as the sun came up one morning, she opened her eyes to see a beautiful blonde woman in a red dress standing beside her bed.

The woman appeared to be pleading with Tina as if to convince her of something, but Tina couldn't hear her words. When the woman saw Tina was awake, she rushed closer, seemingly walking through the bed. At that point Tina had let out a scream, and Kim came rushing into the room.

"What happened?" Kim asked.

"Where did she go?" Tina cried out.

"Who?"

"The woman in the red dress! She was standing right where you are now!"

Kim went to the window and checked the lock. "The latch is closed, and I was right there in the hall when you screamed. No one came out of your room."

Tina slipped out of bed and stood where the woman had been shouting at her. "I swear I saw her . . . "

Kim playfully tugged on her sister's hair. "Was it one of those dancing ghosts from the Haunted Mansion?"

Tina slugged her sister in the arm. "It isn't funny."

Kim rubbed her shoulder. "At least it got you out of bed. School starts in half an hour. Get moving!"

❧

The Layton High Lancers expected to have a great football season. The whole school was rallying around them after they won their season opener against Ogden High by the score of 56-7. However, the Lancers now faced a tough home game against the Logan High Grizzlies, one of the best teams in the state.

Kim and Tina attended the game with Nicole, and they squeezed into the bleachers with the rest of the students. They cheered as loud as anyone when the Lancers pulled out the victory on a long touchdown pass in the final seconds.

However, the real highlight of Tina's night came when Roger Harmer sat down next to her during halftime. Tina felt a tingle in her stomach, and she wished Kim hadn't gone with Nicole to buy some hamburgers at the refreshment stand.

From the first day of school, Tina had admired Roger and his spiked blond hair. They had made eye contact many times during Geometry class, but had never said more than "Hi" to each other. Now he was sitting next to her!

"How did you do on that Geometry test we took Wednesday?" Roger asked.

Tina glanced at him. "I got a 92."

"Whoa! I think I found a new study partner," Roger said. "My score was only 50 points lower than yours. Maybe you could help me out."

"Oh, I don't know," Tina said with a blush. "We'll see."

Kim and Nicole were approaching them, and Roger quickly excused himself. "Well, I'll see you Monday."

Then he moved down a few rows to join a group of rowdy guys as the second half began. Nicole gave Tina an odd look. "What did Roger want?"

Tina just stared ahead nonchalantly. "We have Geometry together, and he wondered how I did on our last test."

Kim stayed quiet, but she had noticed Tina's bright cheeks when they had returned, and thought there might be something going on besides Geometry.

"He's kind of cute, even with that bad hairdo," Kim said.

Tina gave a little gasp, and Kim smiled. "You like him, don't you?"

"He's all right," Tina said quietly. "Nicole, do you know anything about him?"

She nodded slowly. "I've known Roger nearly my whole life. We grew up in the same ward . . . uh, church group."

"He goes to church?" Tina asked. "Roger doesn't seem like the religious type."

Nicole shrugged. "He hasn't come for the past couple of years. He sure is a nice guy, though. I hope he straightens out."

"Well, maybe Tina can get him back on track," Kim said teasingly.

Tina blushed again, and she was grateful when the Lancers returned the second-half kickoff for a touchdown. The crowd went wild and it ended their conversation, but Tina did notice Roger occasionally glancing back at her during the rest of the game. She realized he truly might be interested in more than just Geometry, and she liked that idea!

# CHAPTER THREE

Tina had spent the weekend thinking about Roger. Her feelings were mixed, because after the football game she had seen him in the school parking lot hanging out with some scary-looking people. But he had seemed perfectly harmless when he had sat next to her in the bleachers.

She was eager to see him again, and during lunch Roger suddenly appeared across the table from her. "It was fun to see you at the game," he said.

"Yeah, it was all right," she said. "I'm glad we won."

"Me too," Roger said. "It almost makes me wish I had played this year! But I have too much fun goofing around in the stands and partying after the games."

"I noticed," Tina said.

Roger smiled slightly, then reached across the table and picked up a discarded straw wrapper. "Tina, I have a favor to ask you. I wasn't joking about you helping me with Geometry. I just don't get it."

Tina studied his eyes, and he seemed sincere. If he really did flunk their last test, he could use some help. "Well, I suppose we could get together and go over our assignment."

"Really? That would be great. Where could we meet?"

"How about tonight at the library," Tina said.

It seemed like a safe enough place to meet. She liked Roger, but mixed with her feelings of excitement about being with him came a strange sense of warning.

Roger frowned a little at her suggestion. "The library?"

"It's that place where people read and study, you know?"
Roger laughed. "Sounds good. Do you want me to pick you up?"

"Can I meet you there at seven?" she asked. He nodded, and then glanced at a couple of friends who were calling to him. He tossed the straw wrapper back onto her tray. "See you then."

❧

Tina watched the clock on the wall of the Davis County Library. It was already 7:10. Her family hadn't even blinked when Tina said during dinner she would be going to the library that night. They knew she was an avid reader, and the library was just a few blocks west of their home. She had promised to be home by nine.

At 7:15 Roger cautiously entered the building with his Geometry book in hand. He seemed completely lost, but once he saw Tina, his cool attitude was instantly in place.

"Sorry I'm late," he said. "I got halfway here and realized I'd forgotten my book."

"That's fine," Tina said. "Let's sit at that table in the corner."

They sat side by side, and for the first few minutes Roger truly seemed to be concentrating on the problems. He even got a few answers right on his own. "See? You can do this!" she said.

He smiled, a bit surprised at himself. "I have a good teacher," he said. Tina felt his foot slide next to hers under the table.

They completed that day's assignment by 8 p.m., and they spent the next few minutes talking about some of their classmates. Tina tried to ignore how Roger's arm casually found its way to the back of her chair. Roger had turned to face her, and his knee was touching her thigh, sending butterflies racing through her stomach.

At 8:15 Roger glanced at the clock. "Whoa! Time has flown by. Thanks for all of your help."

"You're leaving?" Tina asked with a frown, knowing she could stay several more minutes. Roger had seemed to enjoy being with her, so his sudden decision to leave surprised her.

"Yeah, my friends will be waiting," he said. "Some of us are going to hang out at the Layton Hills Mall parking lot tonight. Hey, why don't you come?"

"I don't think so," Tina said, feeling strangely uninterested in his offer. "Maybe I could come if I brought my sister Kim and her friend Nicole."

The smile vanished off Roger's face. "Nicole Nielsen? No thanks."

"Why not?"

Roger shifted uncomfortably. "She's a nice girl, but . . ."

Tina nearly made a joke about Roger not going to church, but thought better of it. Instead she said, "I wouldn't count on me coming, but you never know."

Roger brightened again. "Great! We usually hang out in the parking lot below the mall. The cops don't bother us down there. I'll be driving my old red Mustang. You can't miss it."

For a fleeting moment, Tina wondered what Roger's real intentions were. Why would Roger care if the cops could see them? But she pushed the thought aside and waved good-bye. Roger scooped up his book and headed to the door. Tina sighed and browsed the library rows for a few minutes, finally settling on two romance novels to read.

"This is all the romance I'm likely to get," she told herself.

Tina checked out the books, then started walking home with Roger's smile still in her mind. After a few blocks she turned onto a side street and waited at the corner for a car to pass through the intersection. Suddenly the car lurched at her as the driver tried to reach for something in the back seat.

The car's front bumper clipped Tina's right leg and she was thrown onto the car's hood. She hit the windshield then tumbled off, bouncing three times before landing painfully on her shoulder in the gutter. Her purse and books landed a few feet away.

One of her thigh bones protruded through her pants, and blood was flowing from her ear. The car that had hit her pulled to a stop several yards down the street, but otherwise the street was empty. The pain was intense. Then Tina heard a distinct buzzing sound seemingly coming from inside her body. She heard a faint pop, and the pain was gone! She sat up and felt more at peace than she had in a long time.

⌘

"Wow, that was weird," Tina said. She wasn't bleeding now, and her thigh bone had somehow snapped back into place. She resumed walking toward her home and for the first time she saw other people walking along the sidewalk. Why hadn't she noticed them before? One agitated pair were babbling and screaming, neither listening to the other. Other people expectantly stood on porches, as if waiting for the door to open. A few were actually peeking into the windows of a home! It was disturbing.

As Tina reached the corner again, an old man stepped in front of her and blocked her way. He was wearing a double-breasted suit and a hat straight out of the 1920s. "Hey, you forgot something," he boomed at her.

Tina gave him an irritated look and tried to step around him. "Watch out," she said. "I've got to get home."

The old man slapped his knee and cackled, "You don't even know what happened! Turn around, girl!"

He pointed back in the direction Tina had come. She saw a blood-splattered young girl lying in the gutter about twenty yards away. Tina raced in horror to the girl's side, wanting to help her. Then reality hit her as she looked at the girl's face. That was her body in the gutter.

# Chapter Four

Tina stared down at her broken, blood-covered body. Once she realized it was her body, she was surprised at her lack of concern. She now realized her body was just a shell, covering her real identity like a glove. She had once heard a person's soul referred to as a spirit. Is that what she was now?

The accident had partially torn open her body's shirt and showed her stomach. Tina reached down to cover herself, but her hand passed right through the clothing! She tried again and again to pull down the shirt, but she couldn't grip it. She couldn't even feel the cloth!

The old man was watching her, and he let out a loud laugh. "It looks like you're in big trouble!"

"Don't blame me," she said defensively. "This is Roger's fault. If he'd stayed longer with me at the library, this wouldn't have happened."

At the thought of Roger, she suddenly accelerated into the air. She flew above houses and trees and found herself descending into the Layton Hills Mall parking lot. She came to rest within five feet of Roger, who was sitting on the hood of his car, laughing with his buddies. Tina was stunned to see he had a beer in his hand. She instinctively moved forward to talk to him, but instead another spirit rammed into her, knocking her out of the way!

"Hey, this one is mine when he's drunk enough," the spirit snarled.

Tina backed away and saw that Roger and his friends were surrounded by several desperate-looking spirits. Tina recognized only one of Roger's friends—Bart Dotson from school. The other two guys seemed older. Bart had five empty beer bottles at his feet, and he slowly chugged down a sixth one. Bart staggered slightly, and the prowling spirits closed around him.

Two scenes unfolded before Tina. In one view, Roger and his friends were laughing at Bart, while all around her in a second dimension the desperate spirits were yearning for one more drink.

"Oh how I miss a cold beer," one spirit complained. "It's been so long!"

A female spirit had joined the group. Roger had lit a cigarette, and this woman stood right in front of him, trying to grab the cigarette out of his hand. When Roger took a puff, the woman tried to get it into her mouth, too. When Roger blew the smoke out, the woman tried to surround herself in it and breathe it all in. Of course, she didn't have lungs, so the smoke just drifted away. The woman muttered, "Oh, just one more puff! That's all I want!"

Tina was sickened. She had misjudged Roger. She couldn't believe this was the same guy she had studied with earlier that evening.

Tina turned away sadly, wishing she was home. In an instant she accelerated through the air and found herself at the front door of her home. She tried to grab the knob, but it was a wasted effort as her hand passed through it. She cautiously inched her arm forward, and soon she was up to her elbow in the door. She then slowly pushed her face against the door, and it felt like being sucked into a vacuum. She saw every texture of that wooden door as she passed through it.

In the next moment, she was standing in her home's entryway. Her parents were watching TV in the living room, and Kim was doing her homework at the dining room table. Everything seemed so peaceful.

Tina moved in front of the TV and waved her arms. "Mom! Dad! I died! My body is lying in a gutter!"

Her parents' expressions didn't change at all. They just stared right through her at the Fox 13 weatherwoman on the screen.

Tina's frustration was building by the minute. She moved to the dining room, stood behind Kim, and shouted in her ear, "Hey, I need help! I've been hit by a car!"

Kim dropped her pen and sat straight up. She rubbed the back of her neck and whispered, "Wow, that was creepy."

Kim had felt something! Tina was briefly triumphant, but then Kim resumed writing. Tina spent a few more moments trying to get her attention again, but Kim never responded.

A siren approached their neighborhood, and Kim hoped it wasn't for anyone she knew. A minute later, there was a knock on the door. Kim nervously answered it and saw a grim-faced police officer on their porch.

"Are your parents home?" he asked. "I have a message for them."

# CHAPTER FIVE

Kim called to her parents, who joined her at the door. "How can we help you?" Frank asked.

"There's been an accident," the officer said. "Your daughter Tina has been severely injured."

"That's impossible," Kim said. "Tina is at the library."

The officer shook his head slightly. "Tina was hit by a car," he said. "We found her library card in her purse . . ."

Frank could see the flashing lights down the street. "Let's go," he said.

Tina watched this unfold. She rushed to hug Carmen, but her arms passed right through her.

"I'm sorry," Tina cried. "I'm fine! Everything is going to be okay."

The policeman joined the three of them as they hurried down the street to where a crowd had gathered. Tina rushed ahead of them, more worried about her family's reaction to her bloodied appearance than anything else.

The spirit wearing a suit again appeared at Tina's side. "This is quite a commotion you've caused," the man said. "I just died in my sleep. I didn't get any attention whatsoever."

"Go away," Tina told him. "Can't you see my family is suffering?"

He laughed and glided down the street.

Among the crowd Tina noticed a blonde woman in a red dress. She looked strangely familiar. Even more odd, she wasn't watching the accident scene. She was watching Tina. The woman flashed a smile, then glided right through the crowd before vanishing.

"She's a spirit, too," Tina said to herself, suddenly realizing that the woman in the red dress was the same person who had appeared in her bedroom just a few days earlier. It hadn't been a dream!

Tina noticed a lady pacing nervously near the accident scene. A policeman approached her and said, "Mrs. Hunter, please tell me what happened."

Mrs. Hunter threw her hands into the air. "I didn't even see her," she told the policeman. "I reached behind me to straighten a bag of groceries that had tipped over, and I must've swerved. Oh, this is horrible!"

Tina moved next to the distraught woman and tried to comfort her.

"I'm fine," Tina said. "I'm glad to know it was an accident." But Mrs. Hunter just stared in shock at Tina's body as two paramedics tried to revive her.

❧

As Tina's family reached the crowd, Carmen nearly collapsed in agony at the sight of the body. Frank had to catch her from falling. The paramedics were doing all they could to revive Tina, but so far there hadn't been any signs of life.

The paramedics soon put Tina's body on a stretcher and loaded her inside the ambulance. Carmen was allowed to travel with the body, and Tina joined her. Frank and Kim were invited to ride in a police car that followed the ambulance.

On the way to the hospital, Carmen suddenly felt dizzy. Tina shouted in a medic's ear, "My mom is going to pass out!"

He immediately turned to Carmen and said, "You look like you're going into shock. Rest your head against me."

Carmen did as he asked, and Tina scooted close to her mother, trying to offer comfort. Meanwhile, in the ambulance's cramped space the other medic did all he could to revive the broken body.

Tina sat beside him and looked at her body. She saw the bloody face and shattered leg and felt repulsed. She had spent fifteen years in that body, but now she didn't want anything to do with it.

The ambulance soon crossed over the freeway and roared into the Davis Hospital Emergency Room entrance. Tina's body was rushed into a side room and a team of doctors and nurses tried to revive her.

Tina followed along, although she personally thought they were wasting their time. She even told them so. The doctors weren't allowing anyone else into the room, but Tina saw Kim slip unnoticed into a corner. Then Tina heard a low rushing sound that seemed to sweep her up, and instantly she found herself back in her body!

"Oh, the pain!" she cried out. Every part of her body felt covered in burning embers.

"She's back," one of the doctors shouted, and Tina heard the steady beeping of the heart monitor.

Tina moaned and looked for her sister. Their eyes met. Kim rushed out of the corner and took Tina's hand. "Hold on, little sister," she cried. "Don't die!"

Tina felt a terrible pain shoot through her chest. She squeezed Kim's hand a final time, then the heart monitor returned to a steady tone. A nurse shoved Kim back into the corner as Tina popped out of her body again. The pain was gone! She moved toward Kim and tried to speak with her, but Kim was shaking badly as she watched the doctors continue to work on the body.

As Tina huddled close to Kim, a glow descended around both of them, as if someone had switched on a spotlight. Kim didn't seem to notice, but from within the light Tina heard a soothing, glorious feminine voice say, "Tina, come along now. It's time for you to go."

# CHAPTER SIX

Tina looked up into the light, then back at Kim, not wanting to leave her. Tina knew her death was causing Kim great suffering, so she said, "I want to stay here. I don't want to go back into my body, but Kim needs me."

The light grew brighter, and the voice calmly said, "She will be all right. Angels will attend her."

The voice sounded strangely familiar. Tina began to float upward into the light. A radiant female spirit in a white robe was waiting with open arms just beyond the ceiling of the emergency room.

"Come here, sweet Tina," she said. "Let me hold you."

Tina's mind was opened, and she knew this was her grandmother—her father's mother! Frank had never told Tina about his family. He would only say his parents were dead, and that they should leave it at that.

"Grandma Lucille," Tina said excitedly, surprised she knew the woman's name. Tina sensed they had been dear friends before her birth, and she moved into Lucille's arms. It felt so good to touch another person again!

They hugged for several moments. Lucille's love and spiritual energy surged through Tina. They finally parted and looked into each other's eyes.

"I'm here to guide you to the right place, now that your earth life is over," Lucille said.

Her words jolted Tina. Over?

Suddenly a panorama of her life surrounded Tina. Thousands

of images encircled her. It was a collection of her earth experiences. They appeared simultaneously, yet she could comprehend each one. These images actually began in her mother's womb, and she could feel Carmen's love for her. Then every aspect of her life was shown, from the heartaches to the happy times. It truly felt like she and her father were going over the edge of Disneyland's Splash Mountain once more.

Tina also felt the effects her actions had caused over the years. She didn't enjoy seeing how she had often mistreated her family and friends. She realized she had been quite self-centered and now felt a bit guilty.

As the images faded, she found Grandma Lucille standing patiently nearby. "I sure messed up a lot in those fifteen years," she said. "If there is a heaven, I'm not getting in. Is there a chance I can go back and apologize to everyone?"

Lucille smiled. "You overlooked many of your kind actions. You lived a good life."

"I guess I did a few good things," Tina said.

"Those were fifteen years of learning," Lucille said. "You can build on those experiences as you grow and progress here. You won't be returning to your body."

That thought made Tina a little nervous, but she was beginning to like this new world. It was peaceful and filled with light. "What is this place?" she asked.

Lucille pointed back down into the emergency room. "This is the edge of the Spirit World," she said. "Mortality and immortality meet here."

Tina glanced down at her battered body. The doctors and nurses had stopped attempting to revive her, and a sheet was being pulled over her head. Kim was no longer in the room. "They're giving up already?" she cried out in surprise.

Lucille pointed at a clock in the emergency room. It read 11:45. "It was eleven o'clock when you returned to your body and held hands with Kim," she said. "Those doctors have been working on you for quite a while, but your body is too damaged. By the way, time on earth doesn't match up with how things proceed in the Spirit World. You'll get used to it. Let's move on."

Lucille took Tina's hand, and they were propelled deeper into the bright light. Then with a final burst they emerged into a beautiful meadow filled with colorful, unusual plants. They glided smoothly over miles of lush, gorgeous landscape, and soon a small city appeared below them.

Lucille and Tina slowly descended to the ground in front of a large white building. Tina followed Lucille through the door and then down several corridors. Then Lucille stopped in front of a tan door with the number 184 on it.

"Welcome to your new home," she said.

Lucille led Tina inside a spacious room. It reminded Tina of those spacious Manhattan studio apartments she had seen on TV shows. In the center of the room was a circular table with a large basket of the most delicious-looking bananas, apples and pears Tina had ever seen. Oddly, though, she wasn't hungry.

"Do we . . . eat?" Tina asked.

Lucille laughed. "Only if you desire, my dear. Our spirits don't need food to stay alive like we did in mortality. But tasting delicious fruit is a joyful experience, and you may do so if you would like."

Tina reached forward and clutched a bright-red apple. The fruit seemed to pulse in her hand, and as she bit into it, a wave of pleasure swept through her.

"It is wonderful," she exclaimed.

Lucille motioned around the room at a couch and two chairs.

"You'll notice you don't have a bed," she said. "That was an adjustment for me at first, because during the last few weeks of my life I was bed-ridden. Then I died and found as a spirit I'm always full of energy and never have to sleep again. It's such a relief!"

"Does it ever get dark here?" Tina asked.

"No. The light of Jesus Christ radiates throughout the Spirit World."

"Jesus Christ? You mean he's a real person?"

Lucille nodded solemnly. "He is our Lord and Savior. Without him, all would be lost."

Her statement puzzled Tina, and her grandma shook her head sadly. "Oh, Frank," she said softly. "You have failed your daughters."

"Frank?" Tina asked. "You mean my dad?"

"Yes, your father has lost his way in life, and he hasn't taught you or Kim the things he should have. Now you have a lot of catching up to do, and Frank may even lose his soul."

Tina was surprised—her father lost his temper occasionally, but he wasn't evil. "He's a good father," Tina said. "Why could he lose his soul?"

Lucille stayed silent, and the room's entire far wall flickered to life, like a giant video screen. A small, white house appeared in vivid 3-D.

Lucille motioned Tina forward, then gently pushed her against the image on the wall. Somehow they were now inside the scene, standing a few feet from the house's front porch.

The front door opened, and a clean-cut young man in a white shirt and tie walked outside. He called out, "Mom, I'll get the car warmed up!"

"That's my father," Tina said in dismay. He couldn't have been more than 17 years old. He climbed into the car and started the engine. Two younger girls came out and climbed into the back seat. Tina knew she had seen that house before. It was the one in Nephi her father had driven past on their way back from Disneyland! Finally a woman who looked to be in her 40s came out of the house, shut the door behind her, and walked to the car.

"That's you, Grandma!"

Lucille nodded, not taking her eyes away from Frank. The image shifted, and Tina and Lucille floated along as Frank drove the car down the street a few blocks before parking in front of a building with the words "The Church of Jesus Christ of Latter-day Saints" on the front. Tina had seen similar buildings in Utah. It all suddenly clicked for her.

"This church and the Mormon Church are the same thing," Tina said. "But Dad hates the Mormons! This doesn't make sense!"

Lucille touched her shoulder. "It will. Just keep watching."

The family piled out of the car and entered the building. The main meeting room was already nearly full. Tina watched as Lucille and the girls moved to a bench near the back of the room, while Frank joined another teenage boy at a table covered with trays filled with bread and water.

"Where is your husband . . . uh, my grandpa? At work?"

"Actually, your grandpa Samuel had passed away earlier that year and was already here in the Spirit World. You'll meet him soon."

The scene jumped ahead, and Frank was now kneeling behind the table. He recited a prayer asking God to bless the bread in the name of Jesus Christ. Tina had never heard her father say such spiritual words before. After his prayer, he and the other young man handed trays filled with small pieces of bread to some younger boys, who distributed the bread to the group.

The scene faded, and Tina and Lucille found themselves back in front of the video screen. Tina turned to her grandma, feeling very confused. "Dad hates the Mormons, but he *is* one?"

Lucille seemed troubled. "He *was* one. Your father made some serious errors in his late teenage years. He left town and joined the Air Force. He has blocked the Church out of your family's life because he's afraid he'd have to tell you about his past mistakes. This has kept your entire family from progressing spiritually."

Tina was getting irritated. Was it really possible her father would purposely betray her?

"But everything is fine now, right?" Tina asked. "I get to live in this beautiful building and be with you. Who could ask for more?"

Lucille looked away sadly. "Tina, there is so much more. Yes, this place is nicer than earth, but it doesn't compare to where the rest of the family lives. We live in a place called Paradise. I live in a large mansion with your grandpa, and our ancestors live near us. It is glorious, and I'm sad you can't come live with us."

Tina was shocked. "I can't go there?"

Lucille shook her head. "You aren't prepared to cross into

Paradise. You first have to learn what your father should have taught you, and there is also temple work that must be done for you on earth. That might not happen for a long time. I'm sorry, dear."

Tina felt completely deflated after hearing those words. Just moments before she had been very pleased with her new apartment, but now she knew the rest of the family was living somewhere she wasn't even allowed to visit.

"If you live in Paradise, what is this place called?" Tina asked. "It feels like Paradise to me."

"This area has various names," Lucille said. "Some people kindly call it 'The Mission Field,' but you'll also hear it called 'Spirit Prison.'"

"I guess I can understand why," Tina said. A deep sadness rushed through her, and the apartment suddenly felt like a cell. "So this is it?" she asked. "I'm stuck here?"

"Yes, for now," Lucille said. "If your father had lived as he should have, you would already know the gospel plan and would have gone straight to Paradise after your death. But we can't change the past."

"This isn't fair!" Tina said. "I want to live with you!"

"I want that to happen, too. I know who can help you get started. Let's go see your Grandpa Samuel."

# CHAPTER SEVEN

Lucille and Tina exited the building and moved toward a towering dome in the city's center plaza. Other spirits were moving in the same direction. Many of these people also seemed to be "new arrivals" and each had a white-robed escort. Some appeared to be in their teens or early 20s, but most were middle-aged or older. These spirits wore typical worldly clothing, and Tina glanced down at herself. She was wearing the same clothes she'd been wearing when she died—or at least a spiritual version of them.

"Could I have a white dress like yours?" Tina asked.

"Be patient, dear," Lucille said with twinkle in her eye. "There will be a time when you'll receive one, but your clothing is fine for now."

One man in particular caught Tina's attention. He wore a fishing vest, rubber boots and a hat that said, "Fly fishing or death!"

Lucille said, "That's your second cousin Tommy Marlar. He drowned today in the Snake River. Isn't his hat ironic?"

Tina chuckled. "Why would he wear it here?"

"At this stage, the 'newcomers' to this part of the Spirit World usually arrive wearing the spiritual equivalent of what they were wearing when they died, just like you."

In the dome's marble lobby, the escorts mingled and greeted each other. Meanwhile, the new arrivals waited quietly, unsure of what would happen next. Then a soft voice echoed from a hallway, "Welcome! Please come this way!"

Tina looked at Lucille, who signaled she should enter the hallway. "I'll see you soon," Lucille said.

Tina moved down the hall with other new arrivals and found herself next to a teenage girl with short green hair who was dressed in a black leather miniskirt.

Tina smiled at her. "Hi, I'm Tina."

The girl gave her a sideways glance. "I'm Ellen. Do you know what's going on?"

"Not really," Tina said. "I guess we'll find out."

"How did you get here?" Ellen asked.

"What do you mean?"

"You know, how did you die?"

"Oh. I got hit by a car."

"At least you went out with a little dignity," Ellen said with a small frown. "I got stabbed at a party."

Tina recoiled a bit. "Wow. I'm sorry."

Ellen shrugged. "I'm in a better place, aren't I?"

They entered a large room with ten different lines. Each one led to a person operating a computer. Tina and Ellen got in line together, and when they reached the front of the line a woman in a white robe asked Tina for her name.

"Tina Marlar."

The woman typed in her name, and the computer screen was instantly filled with a tree-like chart, with Tina's name on the left side. The chart broke into branches, showing her family line. She recognized the names of Grandpa Samuel and Grandma Lucille. The portion of the chart where her mother's family would be listed was blank.

The woman motioned to the screen. "The chart indicates you are a descendant of members of The Church of Jesus Christ of Latter-day Saints, but you are not a member. Is that correct?"

"Right," Tina said. "I would like to be, though."

The woman smiled and handed her a small card that read *Room Seven*.

"Go to this room, and you will learn more. Next?"

It was now Ellen's turn, and Tina waited for her. When the computer pulled up Ellen's pedigree chart, it was completely blank.

The woman asked her, "What are your desires here in the Spirit World?"

Ellen shrugged. "To have a good time."

The woman raised her eyebrows. "Well, why don't you go with Tina to Room Seven and see if you like the message you hear there. If you don't, other arrangements can be made."

"That's fine," Ellen said.

The woman gave her a card, and the girls soon located the room. It had a high ceiling and held about 100 chairs arranged in stadium seating. The chairs faced a well-lit podium at the far end of the room. Nearly half of the seats were already filled, but the front row was completely empty, so Tina and Ellen sat there.

"Do you know what's going to happen?" Ellen asked.

"I think we're going to learn about Jesus Christ," Tina said.

Ellen rolled her eyes. "Oh, great. All I need is more preaching."

Within moments a large man in a white robe appeared at the podium. Tina instinctively knew he was her Grandpa Samuel. He looked in her direction and gave a brief nod and smile.

"Do you know him?" Ellen asked.

"He's my grandpa."

"Really? I haven't seen anyone yet that I know."

Suddenly the light seemed to get even brighter around Samuel. "Welcome to the Spirit World, my friends," he said warmly. "Most of you are descended in one way or another from Benjamin Franklin Marlar and his wife Mary, who lived in the United States during the 1800s. Let me show you what they looked like."

As Samuel spoke, a glowing cloud-like substance formed a few feet above his head. Inside the cloud was a life-size 3-D color image of the Marlars standing outside a log cabin talking to each other. If Tina hadn't known better, she would've believed they were actually standing right there in the air.

Samuel glanced up at the image. "This couple and their children helped settle the state of Kansas. They now have eight generations of descendants on earth."

That was news to Tina. She'd certainly never met any of them.

"Today I'll explain how the Spirit World works," Samuel said. "It isn't much different than life on earth. We are actually still on earth, but in another dimension or sphere. One big difference you may have already realized is earthly wealth and fame don't help you here. You may have held very important positions on earth, but as you have noticed, 'You can't take it with you.'"

One man wearing a fancy suit called out, "You can say that again! I had five large homes all over the world, and two million dollars in the bank. Now all I get is a crummy apartment? You call that fair?"

"In many ways, it is fair," Samuel said. "Now everything is on an even playing field. The important thing now is whether or not you accept true eternal principles. That will determine your future."

Samuel then explained the role of Jesus Christ in the overall plan. Tina was surprised to learn Jesus had actually helped create the earth, and that his death had been a sacrifice for all mankind. The cloud above the podium showed brief images from Jesus' life. Samuel explained that to live with Jesus again, a person had to accept the principles he had taught.

Then Samuel got straight to the point. "To follow the Savior you need to have faith in him, repent of any sins you may have committed on earth, then join The Church of Jesus Christ by accepting baptism by immersion and being confirmed a member of the Church."

Tina felt a stirring in her heart, and she wished she'd known that before she had died. However, Tina noticed Ellen was acting jittery, and other people shifted in their seats. Finally a man shouted, "That isn't what I was taught on earth! What did you say is the name of this church?"

"On earth, it is known as The Church of Jesus Christ of Latter-day Saints," Samuel said. "Some people call it the Mormon Church."

Those words seemed to spark an explosion as everyone in the room began talking at once. One lady yelled, "I'm a Catholic and will always be a Catholic. Don't tell me those teenagers in white shirts and ties that kept knocking on my door were telling the truth! I don't believe it! I'm going to find the Catholic Church."

She then stood up and marched out of the auditorium. Other people made similar comments. Ellen suddenly stood up as well.

"You can't tell me how to live my life," she shouted at Samuel. "Nobody tells me what to do!"

She turned to Tina and said, "Let's go. He might be your grandpa, but he's crazy."

Tina didn't move. "You can leave if you want, but I think I'll stay."

"You believe this stuff?" Ellen asked.

"Actually, I do."

"You're a fool," she said angrily. "And so is your grandpa."

Ellen suddenly ran right at Samuel as if to attack him, but she never made it. Two white-robed men appeared from seemingly nowhere and grabbed Ellen by the arms. She kicked and screamed, but the men whisked her right out the door.

# CHAPTER EIGHT

Following Ellen's outburst, even more people left the room. Tina looked worriedly at Samuel, wondering if his feelings were hurt, but he stood calmly. It apparently wasn't the first time he'd seen such a reaction. Tina noticed the millionaire was one of the first people to leave.

Once everything settled down there were only about ten people left in the room. Samuel asked them to move together into the seats directly in front of him.

"Thank you for wanting to follow the Savior," he said. "The first few hours after death are when people show their true colors. Many of the people who just left have good hearts, but they still cling to their earthly traditions. Hopefully their hearts will eventually change."

Samuel then said he would explain the earth's history. The room went dark, and images again appeared in the cloud above him. As Samuel talked about Adam and Eve, two radiant people were shown in a beautiful garden, and then being cast out into the world. Soon they had many children, and the human race spread across the earth. History hadn't been Tina's best subject, but now it all fit together so logically.

She was astonished to learn Noah's Ark really had been built, and the Great Flood had actually happened. She watched in horror as millions of people drowned, and was relieved to see Noah's family survive the flood and start anew. The presentation lasted a long time, but the group was engrossed by what Samuel was teaching them. Entire civilizations emerged then passed away.

Then a young woman named Mary was shown. Tina was on the edge of her seat as Mary received a visit from an angel who told her she would be the mother of the Son of God. The group watched shepherds visit Jesus and his parents in a stable. Jesus then grew to adulthood, was baptized by John, gained followers, and taught multitudes about the gospel plan.

Samuel's voice became emotional as he told of the Savior's suffering for the sins of the world in the Garden of Gethsemane. The group watched the crucifixion unfold, and it was painful for Tina to watch the nails being driven into Jesus' hands and feet. Then after several agonizing hours on the cross, the Savior died and his body was put in a tomb.

Tina's gloom turned to joy as she saw the Savior emerge from the tomb after three days. Samuel explained that Jesus had been resurrected. His spirit and body had been reunited in perfect form, and the group was shown many other followers of Jesus leaving their tombs at that time as resurrected beings.

Samuel paused the presentation when someone asked, "How come they got to be resurrected? Don't we ever get to be?"

"Yes, the Savior has opened the way for everyone who has ever been born to be resurrected," Samuel said. "You will all be resurrected someday."

"But when?" another person asked.

"Those who follow the Savior's plan will be resurrected when he returns to the earth in glory," Samuel said. "On earth that event is called the Second Coming, and it is going to happen soon."

He then motioned toward the door. "Unfortunately, many people—like some of our friends who chose to leave earlier today—reject the Savior and his gospel plan. They will have to wait a long time to be resurrected, and they won't receive the eternal blessings and glory that could have been theirs."

❧

As Samuel's presentation continued, he spoke about a man

named Joseph Smith who lived in the early 1800s. Tina had never heard of him, but she watched in amazement as Joseph translated gold plates compiled by an ancient prophet named Mormon. Joseph published their contents to the world.

Tina raised her hand. "On earth, my sister's friend Nicole was always carrying the Book of Mormon around with her. Is that the same book you're talking about?"

"It is," Samuel said. "Members of the Church of Jesus Christ read it to learn more about the Savior's plan. That is also why people sometimes call members of the church 'Mormons.'"

Samuel then spoke of how Joseph restored the Savior's church to the earth. Tina was pleased to see how strong and happy Joseph looked. She had never seen anyone radiate so much goodness and light, other than the Savior himself. But then the group watched in horror as wicked men ambushed a building and killed Joseph and his brother Hyrum.

The group was silent, unable to understand how such a thing could have happened. Samuel said, "When Satan gets control of the hearts of wicked men, unimaginable things can happen."

The presentation continued, and the group saw another man named Brigham Young become the leader of the Savior's church. He guided the church members west across America's plains and mountains, and after a difficult journey they reached a large valley in the desert. They built a community and named it Salt Lake City.

"Hey, I've been there," Tina said. A lady next to her gave Tina a strange look, but Samuel nodded approvingly.

An image of a large granite building with six spires was shown, and Tina recognized it. She had seen it when her family was traveling back from Disneyland. Samuel told them it was the Salt Lake Temple.

Then the group was shown dozens of other temples around the world, and Samuel told them the key to their progression after death involved those buildings. He said special ordinances were performed in the temples for those who had died.

"There are four basic steps you must follow to progress from here to the place known as Paradise. I mentioned them briefly just before the riot broke out," Samuel said with a smile. "First, have faith in the Lord Jesus Christ. He is the Savior of the World, and through His sacrifice we can return to live with our Heavenly Father."

Tina felt a warm sensation in her chest as he mentioned Jesus, and she knew she was hearing truth.

"Second, repent of the sins and transgressions you committed on earth," Samuel said. "You must make a change within yourself. Actually, if you are still here in this meeting it shows you have a good heart and have lived an honorable life. When you died, you may have observed other spirits who seemed chained to earth. In reality, they are chained to their old habits and have stopped progressing spiritually."

Tina thought about the spirits who had tried to get into the body of Roger's drunk friend at the Layton Hills Mall, and the woman who tried to inhale the cigarette smoke.

"When you have firmly committed to living the gospel of Jesus Christ, you can enter his kingdom by being baptized in his name," Samuel said. "In your case, that means accepting a baptism in your behalf in a temple on earth. Following the baptism, someone will receive the gift of the Holy Ghost in your behalf. If you accept these ordinances, you become a member of Christ's church."

It sounded wonderful to Tina. It all fit together. But as she listened to those around her, there was still some mumbling and dissension. One woman said, "I was baptized as a baby. I don't need to be baptized again."

She stood and abruptly left the room as the others had. Amid all the confusion, one man sat glumly. Samuel approached him and asked, "What is troubling you?"

The man looked up, then tears came to his eyes. "I think I rejected the Savior's missionaries last year. I listened to their message, but it seemed like a problem always cropped up when they were supposed to visit me. One time my car broke down, then my son got expelled from school. I liked what I was hearing, but I finally told them I didn't have time to listen. Now I'm dead, and I feel I missed my chance."

Samuel put his hand on the man's shoulder. "You're a good man, and the Lord is merciful. It's too bad you didn't listen to the missionaries, because their message would have blessed your entire family. But we also have missionaries here in the Spirit World. Would you be interested in having them visit you?"

The man's face changed completely from sadness to joy. "There are missionaries here?" he asked. "Yes, send them to me!"

Samuel then he turned to Tina and asked, "Would you like to visit with the missionaries as well?"

"That would be wonderful," she said. "I can't wait!"

"How about the rest of you?" Samuel asked.

Everyone who remained in the room said they wanted to talk to the missionaries.

"I'm proud of all of you," Samuel said. "Now return straight to your rooms and ponder the things I have explained to you. The missionaries will contact you shortly."

The members of the group went their separate ways, but Tina stayed long enough to give Grandpa Samuel a hug.

"It's so good to see you," he told her. "Every day your grandma and I have prayed that you and Kim could stay on the right path, even though Frank hasn't taught you as he should. It looks like you have made it through just fine."

They embraced again, then Samuel said, "Now hurry back to your room. You'll have visitors soon."

# CHAPTER NINE

Tina exited the building and was surprised to see the plaza was now crowded with people. She wasn't sure which way to go when a blonde woman stepped in front of her.

"I can help you," the woman said happily. "Are you going to the Marlar complex?"

"I am," Tina said, glad for the help. The woman was beautiful and wearing a glowing red dress. Tina realized this was the same woman who had appeared in her bedroom and at the accident scene.

"Do I know you?" Tina asked, suddenly feeling uncomfortable.

"I often watched you on earth," the woman said with a smile. "I suppose you sensed me there on occasion."

"Were you like a guardian angel?"

"I guess you could say that," the woman said. "What did you think of the message in there?"

"I thought it was great," Tina said. "It all makes sense to me. I hope to make it to Paradise."

The woman arched her eyebrows. "Really? Look around you! This place is so much better than earth! Do you really think there is someplace better than this?"

Tina was surprised at the woman's words. "Well, Grandma Lucille said she lives in a mansion in a place called Paradise."

The woman suddenly frowned. "Lucille tells that to everybody, but don't believe everything she says. All she did on earth was take care of her children. Does that merit having a mansion? I don't think so. I worked myself to the bone in the business world, and what did I get? A one-room apartment. I don't believe her stories about having a mansion, and neither should you."

"How do you know Grandma Lucille?" Tina asked.

"I'm her cousin Ruby," she said. "Lucille and I knew each other on earth. Anyway, why don't you come with me? I'll show you more interesting things than Samuel's boring lecture."

She pointed down a path to another plaza where people were laughing and dancing to music. It did look fun, but Tina felt she should follow her grandpa's advice to return to her room.

"No thanks," she told Ruby.

"Okay," Ruby said. "Can I accompany you?"

Ruby touched Tina's elbow, and a cold feeling passed through her. Rather than answering her, Tina darted away as only a spirit can. Within an instant she was outside her room. She hurried in, shut the door and suddenly felt very irritated. Ruby was beautiful, and her words sounded inviting, but Tina remembered the cold feeling that had come when Ruby touched her. How could it be possible that Ruby was her guardian angel?

As Tina pondered the strange encounter, a knock sounded on the door. A voice called out, "Tina, dear? Can I come in? Please open the door."

It was Ruby.

# CHAPTER TEN

‿❧‿

Tina opened the door slightly. "Ruby, I don't want to go dancing at the plaza."

"Come on," Ruby said cheerfully. "It will be fun."

There was a rustling in the hall, and suddenly Tina saw a young woman in a white dress standing beside Ruby. "Don't invite her in," the newcomer said. "You'll never get rid of her if you do."

Ruby glared angrily at the other girl. "Mind your own business! I just wanted to show Tina the many attractions we have here."

The young woman ignored Ruby and reached through the doorway. She took Tina's hand, and a warm, pleasant feeling passed between them. "I'm Ida Marlar, also one of your relatives. Tell Ruby to leave. She wants to destroy you."

Ruby's eyes widened. "Why, you lying—"

"Ruby, leave," Tina said, cutting her off. Ruby stopped mid-sentence, and then slowly backed away.

"Ida, I hope they take you away soon," Ruby said. "You've been nothing but a thorn in my side."

Ida's eyes narrowed. "You have no room to talk," she said. "Now get out of here!"

Ruby gave one final glare, then abruptly disappeared down the hall. The gloomy feeling she had brought with her also vanished.

Ida gave Tina a big smile. "I'm glad I made it in time, although from what Lucille has told me, you wouldn't have listened to her."

"Are you my missionary?" Tina asked.

"No, but I'm certainly your friend, unlike Ruby."

Tina opened the door and motioned for Ida to enter. "What

43

did you mean by saying Ruby wanted to destroy me?"

"Exactly that," Ida said. "She wants you to be as miserable as she is and never be able to live in Paradise."

"Why is she so unhappy?"

Ida shook her head. "Ruby made some poor choices on earth and turned against her parents. Her mother lived here in this building before journeying to Paradise, and she told me of the heartache Ruby had brought her on earth. Drinking, staying out all night with strange men … you name it and Ruby has done it. She never married, and spent her life as a secretary. She usually ended up in an affair with her boss, often ruining his life. Then she would move on to another job. After she died, she still had those same dark desires. Satan's followers easily recruited her, and she's been the family pest ever since."

"Hold on," Tina said. "Satan? The devil? He's real?"

"Most definitely! Everything would be so much easier if he didn't exist. He works non-stop to mislead Heavenly Father's children. He's having great success in the mortal world, and his followers are doing pretty well here, too. The difference is he has full reign in the mortal world, but here Satan and his followers are limited to Spirit Prison. He has no power in Paradise."

Tina noticed that despite Ida's youthful appearance, she seemed extremely wise. "Have you been here long?" Tina asked.

Ida gave a sad smile. "Longer than anyone else in this building, but I've accepted my fate."

"I don't understand," Tina said. "Why can't you go to Paradise?"

"I'm just a victim of curious circumstances," Ida said. "I know the gospel is true. I have never doubted it. My greatest wish is to go to Paradise, but I realize I will have to wait until the Millennium to leave this place."

"I don't understand," Tina said. "Grandma told me I would probably get to go to Paradise soon."

Ida nodded. "That's probably true," she said. "I've seen hundreds of Marlar descendants come through here. They move on to Paradise once someone does their temple work. My own parents and siblings live in large mansions across the Great Gulf. It was actually your Grandma Lucille who found their records on earth after she joined the Church. She opened the way for them, but she didn't find my records. She has apologized to me many times, but it isn't her fault."

Tina was getting confused. "What are you talking about?"

Ida patiently put her hand on Tina's. "To enter Paradise, you have to believe the gospel of Jesus Christ with all your heart. Then you either have to be baptized into Christ's church while on earth, or if you have died, someone must perform the ordinances for you in one of the Lord's holy temples. That will probably never happen for me until Christ returns to earth and my status is revealed to someone on earth. Then my work will be done."

Ida moved to the couch, and Tina joined her. "How come it can't happen sooner?" Tina asked.

"I lived on earth in the 1870s. Back then, the Savior's church only had a few thousand members, and they all lived near Salt Lake City. My family lived in a small town in Kansas, and we never heard about the gospel, so naturally I was never baptized. And now no one on earth knows I was ever born, because my parents never wrote down anything about me."

"During Grandpa Samuel's presentation I saw images of Benjamin and Mary Marlar from Kansas," Tina said. "Are they your parents?"

"Yes."

Tina was puzzled. "Everyone seems to know them, but they don't know about you?"

"My parents are well-known throughout the Spirit World, but not on earth."

"Don't they have enough influence to get you into Paradise?" Tina asked.

Ida stood and shook her head. "If you die before age eight, you automatically go to Paradise. For example, my younger sister Martha died at age six, and she went directly there. But I lived from Jan. 11, 1871 to March 15, 1879—just over eight years—and just a little too long to qualify. The Lord's kingdom is governed by laws, and I lived to the age of accountability."

"That seems unfair," Tina said. "Isn't there a way to appeal?"

Ida chuckled a little at Tina's anger. "I'm fine with it. I just look at it as a very long missionary calling—although once I passed the 130-year mark I started feeling ready to move on."

Ida laughed at herself, but Tina was still upset. "We'll sort this out," Tina said.

Ida placed her arm around Tina's shoulder. "It's just the way it is. As I said, I'm just a victim of circumstance. My body is buried in a forgotten grave in Osborne, Kansas. My burial records are there in the courthouse, but no one knows they need to look for me. It's my own fault, I guess."

"What do you mean?" Tina asked.

"Well, I wouldn't have died so young if I'd obeyed my mother, but it was such a beautiful spring day. The prairie grass was just starting to grow, and there was a little spot down by the stream I loved. There was a large, smooth rock I would sit on and let the sun warm me. But that particular day Mother told me to stay in the house. She had a feeling something terrible was going to happen."

Ida frowned a little before adding, "But I sneaked away to the rock by the stream. Unfortunately, I didn't know it was also the favorite place for a large prairie rattlesnake to warm himself. As I climbed onto the rock, the snake was already there. He had a winter's worth of venom in him, and he sunk his fangs into my shoulder. I slumped forward onto the rock and called out to Mother, but she never heard me. Soon my body started going numb, and I couldn't call out anymore. Within an hour I died right there on my favorite rock."

"I'm so sorry," Tina said.

Ida smiled slightly and added, "The frustrating thing is if I had lived just a year longer, my name would have been recorded in the 1880 U.S. Census and my temple work would have been done long ago. But my own disobedience is what has kept me here."

"You can't blame yourself," Tina said. "I'll help you move on."

"I've heard that before," Ida said with a shrug. "You'll probably have your temple work done soon, and then you'll be on your way to Paradise."

"I wouldn't count on it," Tina said. "My parents have never been to a temple, and my dad hates the Mormons."

Ida smiled sadly. "Then maybe we'll be here until the Millennium together."

She gave Tina a final hug, then walked slowly out of the room.

# CHAPTER ELEVEN

⤸✺⤷

Tina was sitting on the couch pondering what Ida had said when Lucille returned. She saw Tina's glum face.

"Ida has obviously paid you a visit," Lucille said. "She's a wonderful girl, and I'm sure you'll become good friends. She just likes to tell her story to new arrivals, and it's a bit depressing."

Tina nodded. "She's been trapped here a long time."

"Somehow we'll find a way to get her into Paradise," Lucille said. "But we'll worry about Ida later. Let's hurry, we're running a little late."

"Where are we going?" Tina asked in surprise.

"To your funeral, of course," she said.

Lucille grabbed Tina's hand and they rushed out of the building. They lifted into the air and soon the countryside rushed below them. Then after a slight bump and a brief blast of light, they were out of the Spirit World and soaring over the city of Layton. The contrast was chilling. Even though the sun was shining, the mortal world felt dark, noisy and unorganized.

They crossed above the steady streams of cars on I-15 and settled to the ground in front of a mortuary. They went inside the building, which was packed with people. Tina saw many of her high school classmates there.

In a corner of the main room, Tina's parents and sister stood beside an open casket. They looked exhausted, but they patiently accepted condolences from a line of visitors. Tina wanted to hug each of them, but she knew she'd pass right through them.

Tina moved toward the casket, anxious to see her body. It had been in pretty bad shape the last time she had seen it, but as she peered inside the casket she was pleasantly surprised. She turned to Lucille and said, "I look a little pale, but the mortician did a good job."

Lucille smiled. "Yes, my mortician didn't do nearly as well on me." Lucille then motioned toward Tina's family. "Go stand next to your mother so you can listen to what the guests are saying."

It was a unique experience for Tina as people she barely knew said kind things about her. David, a guy from her history class, started crying when he spoke with Carmen.

"I can't believe Tina is dead," he said. "She was the only person who talked to me at school. She would whisper little jokes to me. I'm going to miss her."

Carmen pulled David in and gave him a hug. "Thank you for telling us that. We miss her terribly, too."

As other students came by and said similar things, Tina was humbled by their words. She had considered herself very quiet and reclusive, but she discovered she'd been well-liked at school. It almost made her want to go back.

A black-robed priest entered the room and stood behind a small pulpit near the casket. He asked everyone to be seated, and Tina's family took seats on a row of chairs behind him. Tina looked around the room and spotted Mrs. Hunter, the woman who had accidentally hit her. She seemed to be doing better, and Tina was glad she had come to the funeral. Roger was also there, but he didn't seem to be doing as well. Tina sensed he somehow felt responsible for her death.

The priest began speaking, and Tina turned her attention to him. "We are here to honor the memory of Tina Marlar, our daughter, sister, and friend," the priest said. "The family has organized a small memorial service, and at its conclusion we will travel to the Kaysville City Cemetery, where the family has selected a burial site."

The priest announced Kim would speak first. Tina was very interested to hear what her sister had to say. She moved within a few feet of the pulpit so she could look directly into Kim's eyes. Tina saw how completely devastated Kim was. It appeared she hadn't slept in days.

Kim unfolded some handwritten notes tucked inside a blue book, and thanked everyone for coming. "We aren't a very religious family, so Tina's death has left us asking a lot of questions," she said. "We may never know why it was her time to die, but I know in my heart that Tina is still alive somewhere."

"I'm right in front of you," Tina said, waving her arms in front of her sister's face, but Kim stared through her.

"My friend Nicole has really helped me through this difficult time," Kim said. "She gave me a book that teaches many truths about God. A prophet named Alma knew where people go after they die. Let me find what he said ..."

Kim began flipping through the book.

At the mention of Alma, Carmen's expression didn't change, but both the priest and Frank visibly flinched. Tina found their reactions to be very curious. The priest looked like he wanted to jump up to stop Kim, and Frank had grabbed both sides of his chair, causing his knuckles to turn white.

Kim finally found the right place in the book. "Here it is. It says, 'Now concerning the state of the soul between death and the resurrection—Behold, it has been made known to me by an angel, that the spirits of all men, as soon as they are departed from this mortal body, yea, the spirits of all men, whether they be good or evil, are taken home to that God who gave them life. And then shall it come to pass that the spirits of those who are righteous are received into a state of happiness, which is called paradise, a state of rest, a state of peace, where they shall rest from all their troubles and from all care, and sorrow.'"

Kim stopped reading and said, "Then Alma talks about wicked people. He says they will be going to live with the devil." Kim wiped her eyes. "I know Tina isn't with the devil. She was a good-hearted person. But I'm not sure she is in Paradise, because she wasn't religious. I wish Nicole could have been here to tell you more about it, but she had to go out of town to a family reunion. She wanted to stay for the funeral, but I told her I would be all right."

Kim paused and began crying. Finally she said, "Now I wish I had asked her to stay. However, before she left I asked her where she thought Tina was now. Nicole said Tina is probably in a place where she can learn how to follow the Savior, then she can go to Paradise. That felt so right to me! I know Tina is still alive, even if she is just a spirit. Tina, if you can hear me, I want you to know how much I love and miss you."

As Kim sat down, Tina felt overcome with emotion and moved close to Kim, placing her lips on her sister's cheek.

"I love you, too," Tina told her, but Kim was crying and didn't sense Tina's presence.

Tina looked over at her father, and he had a strange look on his face. He seemed both sad and furious. Tina knew he didn't like what Kim had said, but Tina didn't care. Frank's selfishness had already cost their family many eternal blessings. Tina next looked at her mother, who just seemed unhappy and confused.

The priest returned to the pulpit. "Kim, thank you for that interesting message of hope. I also believe Tina is in a better place. I will give a few remarks, then we will close the service and travel to the cemetery."

The priest gave a rousing sermon on earning a heavenly reward, but Tina didn't like his message very much. He said it was God's will that she had died, and now her fate was in God's hands.

Tina frowned. The priest made it sound like God would flip a coin on whether she would be with God or with the devil. His talk felt hollow to her, and the audience didn't seem to like it either. Tina found it interesting that Kim's message was much more accurate than the message from a priest who spent his whole life preaching to people.

Following the service, Lucille returned to Tina's side. "I loved Kim's talk," she said. "Didn't you?"

"Oh yes," Tina said. "It was wonderful."

Lucille took her hand again and they elevated right through the mortuary ceiling, then hovered above the funeral hearse as the casket was wheeled outside. "We'll follow the procession," Lucille said.

Tina hesitated. "I don't like seeing my family so unhappy. I think I'd rather return to the Spirit World."

Lucille gave her a stern look. "Someday your spirit and body will be resurrected, and you'll need to know where your body is."

"That's right. Grandpa Samuel told me about that."

❧

The service at the cemetery was quite short. The priest chanted a prayer, then threw holy water on the casket. Some of Tina's classmates lingered for a few minutes, and Tina was surprised to see Roger slowly working his way toward her parents. She moved over to his side, preferring he would just leave.

Roger approached Frank and stuck out his hand. "Hi, I was one of Tina's classmates. I know this is a hard time for you, but I need to tell you what Tina was doing the night she died. She'd gone to the library to study with me. I left early, and I should've stayed with her, or at least given her a ride home. I feel terrible."

Kim and Carmen looked at the ground, unsure how to respond, but Frank's face turned red in anger. Tina stepped to face her father and shouted, "Dad, control yourself!" Then she turned to Roger and said, "Run!"

Tina's words didn't seem to affect Frank, but Roger immediately darted away. Certainly the expression on Frank's face caused Roger to run as much as Tina's shout did.

Frank took a couple steps forward, passing through Tina, but then he let out a long breath. Frank turned to Carmen and Kim. "Have you ever seen him before?"

"I know him," Kim said. "He and Tina had become friends in Geometry class. She had told me they had talked about studying together."

"How come you never told me that?" he asked. "If they hadn't been studying that night, she'd still be alive. Is he a Mormon?"

Carmen and Kim looked at each other. Frank was acting very strange.

"I think he is," Kim said. "Nicole said he used to go to her church."

Frank mumbled something about the Mormons, and Kim moved away from him, choosing to arrange the flowers near the casket. Soon the three of them were the only ones left at the gravesite, although Tina and Lucille were still hovering around.

Finally Frank said, "Kim, I hate to say it, but I found your talk at the mortuary to be embarrassing. It was pure nonsense."

Carmen exclaimed, "Frank! I can't believe you'd say that!"

Frank spun around and faced his wife. "Did you know that blue book she read out of is the Book of Mormon?"

Carmen looked flustered. "No. But what's wrong with that?"

Frank just shook his head in frustration, but Kim calmly said, "Dad, I know what Nicole is teaching me is true. I now believe in God, which is something I have never learned about in our home. My heart feels so good when I talk to Nicole about her church."

Frank's face turned red again. "Kim, shut up! You don't know what you're saying. If I hear another word about God or the Mormons, I might consider kicking you out of the house."

"Frank, please be quiet," Carmen cried out. "We've lost one daughter, and now you're driving off the other one!"

Kim maintained her calm expression. "It's okay, Mom. You can reach me at Nicole's house. She gave me a key to her backdoor in case this happened. Consider me kicked out."

Kim walked away into the cemetery. Carmen watched her go as Frank stared at the casket. Then Carmen unexpectedly slapped Frank across the face.

"You're not kicking her out—I'm kicking you out," she said angrily. "Don't come home until you can apologize to your daughter!"

Carmen chased after Kim and called out, "Honey, hold on!"

Kim waited for her mother, then they fell into each other's arms. Frank didn't even move a muscle or look in their direction. Carmen and Kim circled back through the cemetery, then got in the car and drove away.

Once they were gone, Frank motioned for the cemetery crew to come forward and lower the casket into the ground. He stood there throughout the entire burial process, and the cemetery crew just worked around him like he was invisible. He even stayed after the flowers had been placed on the grave and the crew was gone. The sun was now low in the sky, and he finally began walking slowly toward the cemetery gate.

Lucille and Tina had stood silently nearby through the entire episode, and now Tina looked worriedly at her grandma. "It looks like my death has shattered the family," Tina said.

Lucille's face was grim, but there was a hint of hope in her eyes as she watched her son walk away. "No, dear. As strange as it may sound, I think your death could turn out to be the best thing that ever happened to your family."

# CHAPTER TWELVE

As the sun set on the horizon, other spirits began to converge on the cemetery. Tina noticed they didn't have the radiance and power that Lucille displayed. In fact, these spirits reminded her of Ruby.

One spirit in particular caught Tina's attention. He hovered above a beautiful new tombstone along the road and looked expectantly toward the cemetery gate. Within a few minutes a white car pulled alongside the tombstone, and a middle-aged woman got out. The moment she stepped onto the grass the spirit immediately began sobbing. "Mother, please forgive me," he cried. "I was foolish and selfish! Don't blame yourself! I shouldn't have done it! I'm so sorry!"

Lucille was also watching him. "I know that young man's story," she said. "His parents spoiled him all his life, but when he turned 18 they told him to get a job. He committed suicide instead. I wish people would realize suicide isn't an escape from their troubles. It only makes things so much worse."

"Is he trapped here?" Tina asked.

"Yes, in a mental prison of his own making," Lucille said. "There is still some hope for him, but he has such a long way to go that he may never reach the heights he could have. Intentionally shortening one's life is a serious mistake with huge consequences. Come, let's go."

They rose into the sky and Tina got a better view of the many spirits who were in the cemetery, as if they didn't know where to go.

"Why do some spirits stay on earth?" she asked. "I saw several spirits trying to get into mortal bodies after I died. And the spirit who first told me I had died was a large, arrogant man who acted as if he owned the street."

"Mortals who choose to focus only on themselves continue to do so after death," Lucille said. "They have the opportunity to advance—just like the boy who committed suicide—as soon as they're able to forget themselves and think of others. But it can take a long time, and it often never happens."

Soon they were zooming across the Great Salt Lake, then over Utah's western desert. To Tina's surprise there were large numbers of people there. It looked like a swarming mass. As they got closer, she saw these weren't mortals, but thousands of spirits who were fighting and trying to hurt each other.

Tina saw one woman call a man terrible names, then she grabbed him by the throat and threw him across the desert. He came right back at her and smashed his fist into her face. Her head snapped back further than seemed possible, and then she straightened up and kicked him in the stomach. Since they were spirits, they couldn't harm each other, but it still looked painful. All around them were similar scenes. Tina could feel the incredible anger these people carried.

"I don't understand why they're acting this way," Tina told Lucille. "They seem so bloodthirsty."

"That's right," Lucille said. "Some of these spirits were among the first to come to earth, and they've been wandering the land for thousands of years. They are carnally minded and have stopped progressing. Their souls have shrunk to almost nothing."

Lucille took Tina's hand again, and they moved back toward the Great Salt Lake. "The spirits you saw in your neighborhood after your death are a bit more advanced, but they still have yet to 'see the light.' Those spirits are the ones that mortals call ghosts or poltergeists. They like to play pranks and put a fright into people."

"What about séances and people who say they talk to the dead?" Tina asked. "I can see now how those type of things could really happen."

Lucille frowned. "A righteous spirit would never participate in such things. When mortals claim to talk to dead people, they are talking to a spirit, but it is usually one of these troublemaking spirits pretending to be someone else. So yes, mortals can talk to the dead, but they would be shocked to find out who they are really speaking with."

"Isn't there ever a time we're allowed to contact our loved ones?" Tina asked. "Can I ever talk to Kim? She's really my only hope of ever being allowed into Paradise."

Lucille smiled kindly. "Heavenly Father's kingdom is a place of order, and contact between the different spheres is purposely limited."

She motioned toward the rampaging spirits. "Those people have rejected the gospel plan, and they no longer follow the laws of heaven. So they can do whatever they want—haunt houses, fight each other, or whatever—but those who follow the Savior obey his laws. Righteous spirits don't contact mortals—or alter the mortal world in any way—unless they are instructed to do so or receive special permission."

Tina was silent, feeling sad she couldn't just pop into Kim's bedroom, tell her to join the Savior's church and then have her do Tina's temple work.

"I have one more place to show you," Lucille said. "There are different levels, even in Spirit Prison. This will make you appreciate your quiet little apartment."

Within an instant they popped back through the veil into the Spirit World. They passed above Tina's apartment building and traveled past the plaza Ruby had tried to get Tina to visit. It was still filled with dancing spirits. The further they traveled, the less organized everything became. There were multitudes of spirits below them, but very few wore white robes. The rest of the spirits wore all kinds of clothing, most of it immodest.

"The ones wearing white robes are missionaries," Lucille said. "As you can see, they are greatly outnumbered. Things can get a little tough in this region."

They traveled even further and hovered above hundreds of spirits dancing on top of a building. A group of men were playing hypnotic music. Tina could feel the music's deadening pulse. The music gave her the same cold feeling as when Ruby had touched her elbow. Then Tina spotted a familiar girl wearing a black miniskirt. She was dancing wildly and seemed to be enjoying herself.

"Oh, no. Is that Ellen?"

"I'm afraid so," Lucille said. "She has given in to the tendencies and attractions she had on earth. Ellen has naturally gravitated to the kind of people she sought out while on earth. The missionaries are trying to talk to her, but it's hard to compete with that kind of entertainment."

Tina felt tears come to her eyes, and she turned away. "I've seen enough," she said, and they zoomed back toward her apartment building. Tina's desire to reach Paradise was burning within her. She was already tired of Spirit Prison.

# CHAPTER THIRTEEN

When they arrived at Tina's building, there was a woman waiting for them in the lobby. The woman was chatting happily with Ida. Tina didn't recognize her, but Lucille immediately approached her and gave her a big hug.

"Tina, this is my daughter Evelyn," Lucille said. "She's your father's sister. We will be teaching you the gospel."

Tina's eyes widened in surprise. "Were you one of the girls going to church when I saw my father as a teenager?"

"Yes," Evelyn said. "The other girl was my sister Teresa. She is still on earth and lives with her husband and three kids in that same house in Nephi that we grew up in."

Tina was thoughtful. "When my dad drove past that house on the way back from Disneyland, there was a woman working in the garden. Was that Teresa?"

"It was," Lucille said. "Too bad your father chickened out. Imagine speeding off rather than talking to your own sister!"

They moved down the hall and entered Tina's room. Evelyn and Grandma sat on the couch, while Tina pulled up a chair across from them.

"I heard about the interesting events at your funeral," Evelyn said. "I haven't seen Frank in several years. I was only ten when he left home. He was always very kind to me, so I have a hard time picturing him being so domineering."

"I think his problem right now is he feels his past is catching up with him," Lucille said. "If Kim finds out Frank was once a Mormon, he'll have to explain why he left the Church. He realizes he doesn't have a good explanation. Yes, he broke a few commandments and lost the influence of the Holy Ghost, but he could still come back to the truth."

Tina was surprised by her grandma's words, because she had pretty much given up on her father. "Dad still has a chance?"

"Certainly, while he is still mortal," Lucille said. "But once he dies his options are limited, because he once knew with all his heart that the gospel was true. He was baptized, held the Aaronic Priesthood, and was even the president of his Teachers Quorum. He used to share the most beautiful testimony each Fast Sunday. But he turned away, and the Lord must deal fairly with someone who had received so much light and knowledge."

Tina shifted in the chair. "I liked what Kim said at my funeral. It was so much better than what the preacher said. He made it sound like I didn't have a choice in where I ended up, but that's not true. So I'm eager to prepare myself for Paradise, and hope that Kim comes through for me."

Evelyn clapped her hands. "That's why we're here!"

Using visual aids on the wall screen, Evelyn explained to Tina that before living on earth, she had lived as a spirit with Heavenly Father. Everyone who has lived on earth are spirit brothers and sisters, and have been given the chance to go to earth and receive a mortal body.

Tina was taught that life on earth serves as a way for Heavenly Father's children to face challenges and respond to them. Tina learned that some people find the gospel on earth, while others—like herself—learn about it in the Spirit World.

Evelyn added, "Jesus Christ will soon return to earth in glory and rule for 1,000 years. Those who have followed Heavenly Father's plan will inherit all that God has."

"That's my goal," Tina said. "But what about all of these other spirits I've seen wandering the earth? Where will they end up?"

Lucille took over the teaching. She explained that there are three kingdoms of glory, known as the Celestial, Terrestrial, and Telestial kingdoms.

"The righteous followers of Christ who join his church through baptism and follow all his teachings will live in the Celestial Kingdom," Lucille said. "Then there is a place for those who are good people but who chose not to follow the Savior's commandments. They will inherit the Terrestrial Kingdom. It will be even more beautiful than Spirit Prison, but nothing in comparison to life in the Celestial Kingdom."

"Is that where someone like my friend Ellen will go?"

Lucille shrugged. "The Savior will be the ultimate judge, but unless she accepts the gospel, that's where she will probably go."

"Wasn't there a third one?" Tina asked.

"Yes, the Telestial Kingdom. It is also a beautiful place of glory, but those who inherit this kingdom are the liars and murderers— like the spirits we saw fighting each other in the desert. All of these spirits will eventually receive a resurrected body, but they will be cut off forever from Heavenly Father and the Savior."

"That still seems like they are getting a pretty good deal," Tina said. "Heavenly Father blesses each of us more than we deserve."

"It certainly seems that way," Evelyn said.

"Can a person progress and jump to a better kingdom if he shapes up?" Tina asked. "I mean, maybe Dad will eventually improve."

Evelyn shook her head. "Once you are assigned a kingdom after the Final Judgment, that is your home. That is why earth life and time in the Spirit World are so crucial."

⁓

Each day Evelyn taught Tina more about the gospel plan, and Tina's appreciation for Jesus Christ grew tremendously. He had paid the price for her sins, and she truly felt badly for the mistakes she had made. Tina's only desire was to enter into the Savior's kingdom through baptism. Her little room was feeling more like a prison cell, and she now better understood Ida's frustration about being stuck there.

One important principle Tina learned was the power of prayer. Lucille taught her that saying a prayer is like sending a stream of light to heaven, where under Heavenly Father's direction the angels can respond to her needs. It was a beautiful concept, and although Tina had never prayed while on earth, she made up for lost time in the Spirit World.

She never felt better than when she was kneeling in prayer. Since Tina never got tired, she would pour out her feelings for long stretches, hoping a way would be opened for Kim to accept the gospel.

At the end of one of their lessons, Lucille surprised her by unfolding a beautiful white dress. "You have accepted the gospel, and this dress symbolizes your desire to be baptized. It is only temporary, and when the day comes that you enter Paradise, you will receive a new dress of your own."

Tina gazed at it with wonder. It wasn't the brilliant white of Lucille and Evelyn's robes, but it was so much better than the everyday clothes she had worn since arriving in the Spirit World. They helped her slip out of her other clothes and into the dress. It felt spectacular, and it shimmered almost as if it were alive.

"Thank you so much," Tina said with joy filling her heart.

There was a knock at the door, and Ida peeked her head in. "I heard you were getting your dress today, and I wanted to see it!"

Tina welcomed her in, and they embraced. "I'm so happy for you," Ida said. "You know what this means, don't you?"

Tina shook her head.

"Now you can join me in the Learning Center!" Ida said. "It's reserved for those who have accepted the gospel, and it's great fun. Do you want to go with me?"

Tina looked at Lucille and Evelyn, and they smiled happily. "You will love it there," Evelyn said. "Soak in all of the knowledge you can."

The four of them came together in an embrace. "I love each of you so much," Tina said, barely holding back tears. "Thank you for teaching me the Savior's plan."

Lucille stepped back and smiled at her.

"No, we want to thank you for being such a willing student. Now we just need to find a way to get both you and Ida into Paradise. Let's all keep praying for Frank to soften his heart so Kim can accept the gospel. I believe she is the key."

# CHAPTER FOURTEEN

⁘

Within moments Ida and Tina were in the Learning Center. Tina's first goal was to unravel her parents' past. Tina asked an assistant to see how her parents had met, and a small screen lowered from the ceiling and hovered in front of her.

The screen came to life, and Tina was amazed to see her parents' lives unfold. She saw her mother as a teenager. Carmen had been a stunningly beautiful girl who looked much like Tina. Carmen had often mentioned that she had grown up in Peru, but Tina hadn't known that her mother had essentially run away from home in her late teens, traveled thousands of miles alone, and then illegally crossed the border into the United States.

Carmen had met Frank later that year in a bar outside of an Air Force base in Texas, and they fell in love within a week. In all the years Frank had traveled the globe, no one had ever mesmerized him the way Carmen did. He didn't want to lose her, and since Carmen didn't have any legalization papers, they drove to Las Vegas the next weekend and were married in a small wedding chapel.

Tina was amazed to see the Lord's hand in their lives. She learned her parents had agreed to be married long before they came to earth, and that Kim and Tina would be their children. Tina saw that if Frank had stayed faithful in the Church, he would have been called to serve as a missionary in Peru. He would have taught the gospel to Carmen's family, and there would have been a spark between them.

The original "Plan A" was for Frank to return to Peru after his mission and marry Carmen, then later help bring her parents to the

United States. But when Frank's choices as a teenager ruined that plan, Carmen was prompted to make her dangerous journey to the United States. Tina saw how angels protected her mother, then guided her into Frank's path—even if it was in a bar.

So while "Plan B" certainly lacked the blessings of the original plan, it had worked out in some ways. The obvious downside of "Plan B" was that Carmen wasn't a member of the church, and her relatives in Peru still hadn't been taught the gospel.

As Tina watched this unfold, she saw an image of the earth that zoomed in on a mountainous region in South America. Soon Tina felt as if she were in a poverty-stricken town, and she entered a rundown home. At the table sat two elderly Peruvians with wrinkled, brown skin and graying hair. Tina instinctively knew these people were her mother's parents, and her heart went out to them. They were obviously living in poverty. Tina could sense that Carmen's departure still weighed heavily on them all these years later. They figured she had been killed.

Tina pushed away from the screen, frustrated at her father. "If only he had stayed true to the gospel, everything would be so much better," she said to herself.

Tina's attention returned to the screen, which now showed a pedigree chart. Tina was able to see videos of her ancestors' lives by simply touching the screen. Her Peruvian ancestors had suffered greatly, often barely able to feed themselves. But as the generations rolled backward, she saw she was descended from the people known as the Incas. The chart indicated that these ancestors were now living somewhere in the Spirit World, but they had never heard the gospel. Tina felt helpless. Somehow she had to find a way to help her family follow the Savior.

❧

Tina often attended worship services with Ida. These were special meetings for those who had accepted the gospel but whose temple work had not yet been done.

"I'm the all-time record holder around here," Ida told Tina with a laugh. "I haven't missed a meeting in more than 130 years!"

Ida introduced Tina to a group of distant relatives who had lived in the mountains of Tennessee in the 1890s. Like Ida, many of them had been waiting for more than a century to move on to Paradise.

One of the women excitedly said, "We've got great news. As you know, one of our descendants has joined the church and is attending BYU. She has been in a family history class and discovered us in an old book of Tennessee records. We've received word that she submitted our names to the temple, and our baptisms will be done very soon!"

Ida congratulated them, and the meeting was devoted to this family's imminent departure to Paradise. They shared their testimonies, and they each thanked Ida for her friendship over the years.

Ida was sincerely happy for them, but afterward she told Tina, "It feels like I keep taking second place in a cow milking contest. I'm never going to win the prize."

Soon a message arrived that this group's baptismal work would be done in the Provo Temple within the next few minutes. Tina and Ida embraced each member of the group and enviously bid farewell as each person slipped through the veil, departing to witness their own baptism and confirmation.

However, several of the men returned within a short time. They looked very disappointed to still be in Spirit Prison. One of them explained, "The Young Men's President of the ward doing the baptisms had to work late, so not all of the young men found a ride to the temple. We have to wait until tomorrow. The rest of the group has crossed over into Paradise."

Tina offered her condolences to them, but she secretly thought, "At least you get to go tomorrow! What about Ida and me?"

# CHAPTER FIFTEEN

Tina knew her eternal fate now rested in Kim's hands. Sadly, Kim's fate rested in Frank's hands. Things didn't look too good, but Tina continued praying as often as she could.

Lucille soon visited Tina. "I'm here to let you know your prayers have been answered," she said.

Tina was surprised. "Do you mean Kim is going to be baptized?"

"Not yet, but our family's Governing Council has agreed to listen to any ideas we might have about how to influence your father. They are waiting for us. Let's go!"

"Shouldn't they already have the answers?" Tina asked, but Lucille rushed her out the door, and they soared once again into the air. Soon they were flying above parts of the Spirit World that Tina had never seen. There were magnificent gardens and spectacular fountains. In the distance appeared a dazzling blue ocean.

"Is that the Great Gulf?" Tina asked.

"Yes, and just beyond the horizon is Paradise."

"Oh, how I wish I could see it! Can't we just zoom over and back?"

Lucille laughed. "Someday, my dear. But it isn't that easy. You must pass by the angels, and they know your status."

Lucille pointed ahead, and Tina suddenly noticed hundreds of large angels patrolling the ground and sky along the edge of the Great Gulf. "Wow, they look powerful," Tina said. "I'm glad they're on our side."

Tina felt at peace. Even if she had to wait many years, she was determined to make it to Paradise.

"Grandma, did you know when Ruby talked to me, she told me not to listen to your stories of Paradise?" Tina asked. "She claimed it was all a lie."

Lucille's face clouded with anger—the first time Tina had seen that emotion in her.

"Ruby is a wicked woman," Lucille said. "I tried to help her in mortality, but it was no use. It's sad to see she won't change. Of course Paradise exists! You'll be there with us someday."

Lucille slowed her speed and pointed to a large domed building that had been built along the shore of the Great Gulf.

"There's the Council Chambers," Lucille said, and the pair descended into a large garden near its doors. The garden was filled with radiant, happy people. Lucille and Tina were greeted kindly as they moved toward the building.

"These people are about to begin their missions," Lucille said. "On earth, as the Church of Jesus Christ spreads across the earth, many records in Asia and Africa are now being found and submitted for temple work. A great missionary force has been called here to teach the people whose work will be done on earth."

"How wonderful," Tina said. "I'm always amazed at how organized everything is here."

Lucille led Tina into the building, which radiated a powerful, soothing light. Lucille motioned her into a spectacular golden room. On the far side of the room several men sat behind a long marble table. Tina studied them silently while the men concluded a matter of business. They all wore white robes and looked very distinguished, but they were a curious mixture of age, size and facial hair. A few had bushy beards, two had mustaches, and the rest were clean-shaven. A gray-haired, clean-shaven man seated at the center of the table took the lead.

"Welcome, Sister Marlar," the man said to Lucille. "Who is your guest?"

Lucille stepped forward. "Hello, Brother Dalton. This is my granddaughter Tina. She has recently returned from the mortal world."

"We are pleased to meet you," Brother Dalton said.

With Lucille's encouragement Tina moved forward to shake hands with each of them. Then she returned to Lucille's side in the center of the chamber as Brother Dalton motioned for Lucille to continue her remarks.

"The council is aware that my son Frank left the Church as a young man," she said. "It has been hard for me to see his daughters raised without a knowledge of the gospel. Tina is Frank's youngest daughter, and she might be the key to bringing Frank back into the fold."

Brother Dalton turned his gaze toward Tina. "What do you propose to do?"

Tina sensed this man held great power in the spirit world, so she carefully selected her words. "My fondest wish is to join my grandparents and other family members in Paradise, but my progression is halted until temple ordinances are performed for me."

Brother Dalton merely nodded, so she continued. "My sister Kim is the only true hope for our family. She is very interested in the gospel, but my father is stopping her in every way he can. At my funeral my parents got into a big fight because Kim's friend Nicole is sharing the gospel with her. My family is breaking apart."

Then Tina paused as a flash of inspiration came to her. "So I humbly ask that I may return to earth and do all I can to influence my family to choose righteousness, especially my father."

Brother Dalton smiled. "It's a worthy desire," he said. "Please step outside while we discuss the matter as a council."

Tina and Lucille stepped out of the chamber, and the room's heavy door was closed.

"You did very well," Lucille said.

"I hope so," Tina said. "That idea came out of nowhere."

"I feel it was inspired," Lucille said.

As they waited, Tina said, "I was nervous in front of Brother Dalton. I felt a strong spiritual power radiating from him."

Lucille smiled. "Brother Finity Dalton is one of the great ones.

In mortality, he recognized the truth of the gospel in the 1860s, and he led his family from England to the Rocky Mountains. His descendants have helped the Church grow throughout the world. Brother Dalton is Grandpa Marlar's cousin, and he has presided here in the Spirit World for more than a century, always making wise decisions. I specifically asked him to preside at this council. I was pleased he accepted. He will carefully consider your request."

Just then the door attendant called to them, and they returned to the main chamber. Brother Dalton motioned for both of them to stand in front of him.

"Tina, we can see the wisdom in allowing you to work in your family's behalf," he said. "However, we also must make sure your family members continue to develop faith. Seeing an angel at this point wouldn't help them in the long run. Therefore, we can't allow you to directly affect their lives through a visitation, or cause anything out of the ordinary to happen in the mortal world. If such an incident happens, your assignment will end immediately. Do you understand?"

Tina nodded. "I do, sir."

Brother Dalton looked at his fellow council members. "With that said, I propose the council grant Tina's request. All in favor?"

Each man in the council room raised his right hand, and Brother Dalton smiled.

"Your request has been granted," he said. "Sister Lucille, please escort Tina to the mortal world and give her further instructions as you see fit. This council stands adjourned."

The men stood up, and Tina moved forward to clasp Brother Dalton's hand. "Thank you so much," she said. "This means everything to me."

He grew serious for a moment. "Just do your best. I hope as much as anyone that you can help get your father back on track."

Lucille approached them and put her hand on Tina's shoulder. "Are you ready?" she asked.

Tina smiled. "Let's go!"

# CHAPTER SIXTEEN

It was dark when Tina and Lucille returned to Layton. Lucille guided Tina under the street lamp in front of the Marlar home, where she spent several minutes giving advice on how to best influence Frank.

"Be as subtle as you can," Lucille said. "Anything out of the ordinary will really make your father paranoid. He pretends to not be religious, but for all of these years he's been looking over his shoulder, waiting for lightning to strike him."

"I'll keep that in mind," Tina said.

Lucille gave Tina a quick hug and said, "I wish I could stay, but you'll mostly be on your own. I'll try to check on you once in a while, but the council has asked me to help out with new arrivals in Paradise. With all these new temples being built, the number of spirits moving to Paradise is really starting to grow."

"Well, that's a good thing, isn't it?" Tina asked.

"It is, and my greatest wish is to take you on a tour of Paradise. So do your best! I'll see you soon."

"Thanks, Grandma." Tina then moved toward the house and paused on the front porch to wave good-bye to Lucille, who was slowly vanishing into the night.

Tina cautiously slipped through the front door. In the past, her father would be settled into his easy chair to watch the local news, but tonight the house was dark and silent.

Tina first checked her parents' bedroom. Carmen was alone in bed, staring at the ceiling. It was obvious Frank hadn't ever apologized for his strong words after the funeral. Carmen then turned over, covered her head with a pillow, and let out a small sob of despair.

"I'm here, Mom," Tina said. "I'm going to make things better for our family."

But Carmen didn't move, and Tina let herself float through the ceiling into Kim's bedroom. The light was still on, and Kim was lying in bed reading a small white book about the history of the LDS Church called "Truth Restored" by Gordon B. Hinckley. Kim's face showed deep concentration, and Tina watched her eyes dart across the pages.

Tina observed her sister for several minutes, wondering how to prompt her, but Tina realized nothing could be better than to have Kim reading about the gospel. Besides, she felt as if she was intruding, so she left the house in hopes of finding her father. She figured he was probably staying at a nearby hotel, and she spent most of the night checking for Frank's blue Ford Taurus in the hotel parking lots around Layton. There was no sign of it.

After checking a final hotel, Tina noticed a distant light on the mountain to the south. It was more than just a light—she sensed it was some sort of spiritual haven. She raced toward it and saw a white building bathed in light. It had an architecture similar to the buildings in the Spirit World, and a feeling of goodness and glory radiated from it. The words "House of the Lord" and "The Bountiful Temple of The Church of Jesus Christ of Latter-day Saints" were chiseled into one wall.

As Tina approached the temple she was intercepted by a large man in flowing robes. He had dark hair and Native American features.

"What are you doing here?" he asked politely but firmly.

"I felt drawn to the temple," Tina said. "Could I just go inside until sunrise?"

The man reached out and touched her dress. "This material

indicates you are a follower of the Savior, but you still haven't been to Paradise. Am I right?"

"That's true," Tina stammered. "I have accepted the gospel, but my temple work hasn't been done."

"Then how come you aren't in the Spirit World?" the man asked. Tina sensed he didn't completely believe her.

"I have permission to be here. In fact, I'm looking for my father, but I'm waiting until daylight to find him."

"Who gave you permission?" the man asked.

"Brother Finity Dalton."

He pondered her words for a moment, then seemed satisfied. He extended his hand. "My name is Aaron."

"I'm Tina," she said with relief, shaking his hand and feeling pleased to make a new friend. "Are you guarding the temple?"

"Yes," Aaron answered. "I supervise an army of warrior spirits. We guard the temple. You never know when Satan's armies will attack."

"Really? It seems so peaceful here." Tina looked around, and for the first time she noticed dozens of other angels stationed around the temple grounds.

"You'd be surprised," Aaron said. "This the holiest place in the valley, but it is also one of Satan's favorite targets."

Tina found herself admiring his striking features. "You seem different," Tina said. "You aren't like the other spirits I've met."

"I suppose not," Aaron said pleasantly. He went to a flower bed and stood in front of one of the spotlights that was shining on the temple. His shadow appeared on the temple wall. When he stepped aside, the shadow disappeared.

"How did you do that?" Tina asked in amazement, moving in front of the light herself, but no shadow appeared. "See? Light passes right through me."

"I've been resurrected," Aaron explained. He reached out and shook the trunk of a small tree in the flower bed to show he had a tangible body.

"But I've been taught that no one will be resurrected until the

Savior comes again," Tina said.

"That's true. I guess I'm older than I look," Aaron said with a grin. "I was born in this land just a few years after my grandfather Lehi led our family out of Jerusalem. I died 500 years before the Savior's birth, and I spent the remaining time until his resurrection in Spirit Prison—along with everyone else who had ever lived on earth. It wasn't very enjoyable. It was beautiful, of course, but we felt trapped—unable to progress until the Savior completed his work."

"What did you do while you waited?" Tina asked.

"We stayed busy building cities, preparing for the future," Aaron said. "Even then, there was a division between the righteous and the wicked. Those of us who believed in Christ kept to ourselves along the shores of the Great Gulf, while the millions of other spirits spread throughout the far reaches of Spirit Prison. Then after the Savior's death, He visited the righteous in the Spirit World and led us across the Great Gulf into Paradise. He stayed with us while his body lay in the tomb in Jerusalem and taught us how to organize the missionary program throughout the Spirit World."

"So how did you get a resurrected body?" Tina asked.

"After the Savior was resurrected, we were allowed to return to earth and be resurrected ourselves. We were even able to appear to some of our descendants. Then those of us who had been faithful on earth were called to teach the gospel in Spirit Prison to those who hadn't heard it during mortality."

"So you were one of those first missionaries?"

"I was," Aaron said humbly. "It was an exciting time."

"I hope to get to Paradise myself someday," Tina said. "That's why I'm on earth right now—to help my family accept the gospel, and hopefully have my temple work completed."

Tina and Aaron talked for the next hour, and Aaron sympathized with her difficult circumstances, especially when he learned her father had shirked his duty to teach her the gospel.

As the sun began to rise, cars began to drive into the temple parking lot, and people began entering the temple. Suddenly Aaron looked out across the Great Salt Lake. "Tina, go stand against the temple," he ordered.

Aaron rose into the air and let out a shout. In an instant hundreds of white-robed warriors surrounded the temple, and just in time. Coming from the west were thousands of spirits that can only be described as demons. They looked horrendous. Many demons surrounded each mortal that was walking toward the temple, determined to tempt the person from entering. Others aimed straight at the temple, trying to penetrate the walls, but Aaron and his partners were very skilled at fighting off these demons.

It was actual hand-to-hand combat, and the demons took the worst of it. It was as real as any battle Tina had ever seen, except there wasn't any blood. Meanwhile, the mortals continued to drive up and walk into the temple, unaware of the holy war being waged all around them.

A demon slammed hard into Tina, sending her reeling, then stood above her and laughed, ready to pummel her again. But as he raised his arm, Aaron swooped in, grabbed the demon by the waist, and hurled him several hundred yards.

"Thanks," Tina said weakly. Aaron helped her up, and they watched the demons retreat back into the desert. Aaron looked as exhausted as a resurrected person could, but he gave her a smile. "You got to see quite a show," he said.

"I'm still shaking," she said. "Those demons were frightening— and brutal."

"We had an idea they were planning an attack, because this morning several temple marriages will be performed," Aaron said. "The demons hope to cause the soon-to-be bride or groom to question whether they are doing the right thing. If the demons can somehow disrupt a wedding, they feel they've destroyed an eternal family. But we fought them all off today. In fact, their success rate is terribly low. Satan can't be pleased with them."

It had turned into a beautiful morning, and Tina knew she had to find her father. She thanked Aaron for keeping her company, then she headed back toward Layton. Frank had probably arrived at Hill Air Force Base to start his work shift.

∽

Just a few months earlier, Frank had offered to show Tina the building where he worked, but she had declined. At the time, she figured it would be like all of the other buildings on all of the other Air Force Bases where he had worked. Now she wished she'd taken the offer, because it could take hours to find him. But as she flew over a grocery store parking lot a few blocks south of the base entrance, she stopped in midair. There was his car!

Tina could see Frank sleeping in the back seat. It hurt to see her parents' marriage reduced to this level. She slipped through the car's passenger door and sat in the front seat, waiting for him to wake up. Within a few minutes, Frank's watch let out a piercing beep.

"Carmen, are you all right?" he asked groggily before shutting off the watch. He sat up and looked out the window, then put his hand on his forehead. "Oh, Carmen. What have I done?"

Frank climbed out of the car, stretched, and tucked in his wrinkled shirt. It looked like he'd worn the same clothes for several days. Tina couldn't smell anything in the mortal world, but just by looking at him, she could tell Frank needed to take a shower.

Frank finally got into the driver's seat and drove the car slowly out of the parking lot. He turned on the radio and started singing along to a country song with the chorus, "Going through the Big D, and I don't mean Dallas." Tina listened to the lyrics and realized the song was about a man getting a divorce. She was horrified to hear her father sadly singing along.

"You and Mom aren't getting divorced," she cried out. She instinctively punched a button on the radio to one of her favorite stations, and to her surprise it worked! Suddenly an upbeat dance beat blasted from the car's speakers. Frank sat up straight, then banged a fist on the dashboard.

"Don't tell me you're acting up again," he said to the radio. He quickly hit the button for the country station and continued singing along as he turned into the Hill Air Force Base entrance.

Tina was barely able to contain her excitement about changing the station, and after a few moments she again hit the button to her favorite station. The dance beat blared again, and Frank slammed on the brakes, nearly sending himself through the windshield. He stared at the radio until the driver of the car behind him honked. He looked in the rearview mirror, then slowly pulled the car to the side of the road. Tina couldn't help smiling as her father nervously watched the radio. She could almost read his thoughts: *That's Tina's favorite station.*

He cautiously pressed the button again for the country station and stayed parked along the side of the road through another entire song before finally pulling back onto the road. Tina noticed her father was quite flustered, so she said, "Sorry, Dad. I didn't mean to shake you up."

She left the radio alone the rest of the way, but as Frank pulled the car into his parking stall, she just couldn't resist hitting the button one more time. As an upbeat song blasted from the speakers, Frank slammed on the brakes, squealed the tires and made the car do a little hop.

A co-worker on the sidewalk turned to look at the skid marks on the asphalt as Frank drove the car the remaining three feet into the stall. He turned off the car, hopped out, and quickly slammed the car door as his co-worker gave him a worried look.

"Hey, Marlar, are you all right?" the man asked.

"I'm fine," Frank sheepishly said. I thought I'd just check the brakes. They seem to be working, don't you think?"

His co-worker laughed. "There's no doubt about that."

As Tina followed her father to his work area, she felt a pang of guilt, knowing her radio stunt had already crossed the line of being "subtle," as Grandma Lucille had put it.

Frank went right to work methodically inspecting an airplane. She could tell her actions had shaken him up, though. He would stare blankly for several seconds at a bolt or a tool, and he even muttered once, "That was just weird!"

Finally at around noon Frank went into his supervisor's office. "Ray, I'm really not feeling well," he said. "I'm nearly done checking the plane's left wing, and I'll finish the rest of the inspection tomorrow."

"That's fine," Ray said. "How are you coping with things since the funeral?"

Frank rubbed his face. "To be honest, not too well. Carmen and I are separated."

"I'm sorry to hear that," Ray said. He came out from behind his desk and put his hand on Frank's shoulder. Then for the first time in her life, Tina saw her father shed a tear.

# Chapter Seventeen

After a few reassuring words from Ray, Frank went back to the airplane, checked a few more bolts, then started cleaning up his tools. He had been using a pan of solvent to clean the grime off some of the engine parts, and as he turned to dispose of it, the pan slipped out of his hand. It hit the ground, splashing solvent along his right leg. Frank's eyes grew wide as he saw a co-worker's carelessly tossed cigarette just a few feet away. "This is a 'no smoking' zone," he muttered. If the solvent vapors reached that cigarette . . .

*Whoosh!* A stream of flame shot across the room, and in an instant Frank's pant leg was on fire with flames as high as his face.

"Ray, help me," he yelled. Frank tried to pat out the flames, but he only succeeded in burning his hands. Ray rushed through the doorway and shouted, "Drop to the ground!"

Frank did so, and Tina watched helplessly as Ray grabbed a nearby tarp and smothered the flames. As they pulled the tarp off, Frank took one look at his leg, then covered his eyes. His pants were burned off below the knee, and much of the skin on his calf was gone. "Now I really don't feel good," he told Ray, before closing his eyes in pain and shock.

Ray immediately called the base's medical personnel, who treated the leg the best they could, but they knew the burns were too serious for them to treat at the base hospital. A medical technician told Frank, "We've got to get you to Salt Lake immediately."

Soon the base's ambulance arrived at the building, and the medics loaded Frank inside. Tina had stood by worriedly during all of the excitement, and now she slipped into the ambulance.

These ambulance trips were becoming much too common in her family.

Frank was taken to the burn center at the University of Utah Hospital. Tina stayed by her father's side as he was treated and finally placed in a private room. Frank was drifting in and out of consciousness because of the pain pills. Tina came to his side and placed her hand on her father's face.

"Dad, you're handling this the wrong way," she said. "Call Mom and work this out."

She told him this over and over, and each time Tina told him to call home, Frank would turn and look at the phone. After nearly twenty minutes of Tina's pleadings, Frank finally picked up the phone and dialed. After a moment he said, "Hello, Carmen. It's nice to hear your voice."

Frank paused as Carmen shared her relief that he had called her. He took a deep breath, trying to keep his voice calm despite the severe pain shooting through his leg.

"I've missed you, too," he said. "Hey, I was wondering if you could pay me a visit. I've been admitted into a hospital in Salt Lake."

He listened to Carmen's frantic response, then he said, "No, I'll be all right. I just burned my leg at work, but I wouldn't mind a visit."

Tina could faintly hear her mother's frightened words, and Frank said, "Calm down, okay? I look forward to seeing you."

Frank gave her directions and hung up the phone. Despite the pain he was suffering, Tina noticed a faint smile cross his face.

⚘

Carmen and Kim arrived at the hospital within an hour. At first, the conversation flowed freely as Frank told them all the details about the accident. Then the conversation became forced as the reality of their situation became apparent. They hadn't spoken to each other in nearly two weeks.

Finally Carmen said, "Well, I guess we better go. I'll call you tomorrow."

After a few moments of silence, Frank said, "The doctors think I could probably check out of here tomorrow, as long as I have a place to keep my leg elevated. It could take a few weeks to heal, but I won't get better very fast if I keep sleeping in the back seat of the Taurus."

"Frank, I can't believe you," Carmen said in surprise. "I figured you were at least staying in a decent hotel. You stubborn fool!"

Frank smiled. "If I can come home, I'll behave myself." Then he lowered his voice and said, "Kim, I'm sorry for how I acted at the cemetery."

Kim came forward and kissed his cheek. "Apology accepted," she said.

<br>

On her way out, Carmen consulted with the doctor, who agreed to let Frank return home the following day. Tina considered returning to the Bountiful Temple, but instead she chose to spend the night at her father's side. In the evening, the nurse gave Frank some medication and he quickly fell asleep, hardly even stirring. Tina was glad he was able to rest, and at around midnight she took a stroll through the hospital. She found it interesting that most of the patients also had spirits attending them.

As she rounded a corner on her way back to Frank's room, she watched a touching scene as several spirits descended through the ceiling into an elderly woman's room. A radiant male spirit reached out to the woman and said, "Fern, it is time to come home."

The woman sat up, opened her eyes wide and gave a joyful cry. "I've waited so long," she said.

Then her spirit slipped out of her body, and she joined the relatives who had come to greet her. She looked so young as a spirit compared to her mortal body, which slumped back onto the bed and nearly fell onto the floor, but none of the spirits noticed. They were too busy hugging and greeting each other. Meanwhile, a nurse peeked into the room, noticed the lifeless body, and let out a shout. It was curious for Tina to watch the two scenes—a happy reunion near the ceiling, and a frantic medical staff below trying to revive the woman.

After a few moments, the male spirit told Fern, "Let's go now. The rest of the family is waiting to see you."

Fern took a brief look back at the medical staff working on her body. "They might as well give up, because I'm not going back," she said with a laugh.

Then the group floated through the ceiling and disappeared. Tina pondered how calm the woman had been as she died—almost as if she knew those spirits would be there waiting for her. Her own death certainly hadn't been that peaceful.

∾

Carmen picked up Kim from school so they could go get Frank at the hospital. Their conversation soon turned serious. "Mom, how long are you going to let him stay?" Kim asked.

Carmen stared ahead and finally said, "As long as he wants."

Kim wiped away a tear. "I was hoping you'd say that. Dad has been unbearable lately, but I love him. Doesn't life seem empty without him?"

Carmen nodded. "Your father's a good man, and we need him in our lives. I know you've been talking with Nicole about her church, but let's give it a rest for now. I think our family is more important."

Kim nodded, then carefully shifted her math book to cover up the Book of Mormon she'd been reading every chance she got.

∾

Once they arrived home from the hospital, Carmen and Kim managed to help Frank hop on one leg into the living room. Once he was positioned on the couch with ESPN's Sports Center on TV, he was content to just lay there and let his medication take effect.

Tina had traveled home with the family, and she noticed the Book of Mormon in Kim's pile of books. After Frank was in the house, Kim returned to the car, grabbed her books, then went to her room. Tina hoped Kim would quickly finish the book and be converted very soon.

Instead, Kim hid the book under a pile of papers on the desk and turned on her computer, opening up a computer program that helped design internet webpages. Within moments a partially finished webpage came onto the screen. In the center of the page was Tina's recent school picture, and below it read the words: *Tina Marlar, a true angel.*

A flood of emotion passed through Tina as she sensed how badly Kim was still hurting over her death. She appreciated the effort her sister was making to preserve her memory, but on the other hand, Tina felt there were more important things Kim could be doing with her time. Tina wrapped her arms around her sister and said, "Don't worry about me! I'm fine! Worry about yourself!"

❧

Kim sat straight up in the chair, and her hair stood on end. It felt like somebody had just squeezed her and whispered in her ear. She stood up and cautiously looked around the room. "Who's there?" she asked.

Tina moved above Kim's bed, pleased to have been felt, but she was concerned at her sister's reaction. Kim went to the bedroom door and called out, "Mom, can you come up here for a moment?"

As Carmen came up the stairs, Kim asked, "Is someone else in the house besides you and Dad?"

"No," Carmen said, sensing something was really bothering her daughter. "Tell me what happened."

"Well, I started working on my memorial for Tina, and suddenly my whole body tingled and I thought I heard a voice."

Carmen gave her daughter a smile. "Maybe you're just tired. It's been a long day. Dad is drifting off to sleep and I doubt he'll wake up again for a while. Why don't you go kiss him goodnight?"

Kim nodded and left the room. Carmen followed, but she paused to look back into the room. She had been purposely cheerful for Kim's sake, but she had also felt a presence in the room.

As a young girl in Peru she had felt similar sensations. Her grandmother had told her these feelings meant she was in the presence of a dead person. There was no mistaking it this time. She could sense a spirit hovering above Kim's bed, then it darted out the window. It never dawned on Carmen this spirit could be her daughter. In her mind, Tina was somewhere in heaven—likely playing a harp.

Carmen stood in the doorway for several seconds, then softly said, "Whatever you are, stay away from my family."

# CHAPTER EIGHTEEN

Carmen woke up grumpy. She had spent the night worrying about the "spirit problem" in Kim's room. Once Kim had gone to school, Carmen slipped back upstairs. At that moment, Tina happened to return to the room after spending the night at the Bountiful Temple visiting with Aaron.

Carmen walked cautiously toward the center of the room. "I can feel you," she said nervously. "You just came in, didn't you?"

Tina was surprised by the tone in Carmen's voice. Tina knew that Kim had been shaken up last night, but she had no idea Carmen was feeling the same way. Tina had purposely left the house after Kim sensed her, rather than have the council accuse her of meddling in the mortal world. But Carmen's nervousness confused Tina, and she floated next to her mother. It backfired terribly as Carmen punched wildly at the air and said, "Get away from me!"

Carmen stumbled back against Kim's desk, jostling the papers. Tina returned to the upper corner of the room, stunned at her mom's response. "I just want to know if you are a good spirit or an evil one," Carmen said as she moved to the center of the room. Tina was stunned to realize Carmen had never considered the spirit might be her.

When Carmen had bumped the desk, it had partly uncovered the Book of Mormon that Nicole had given to Kim. Tina noticed the book, and was torn between trying to cover the book again, or drawing Carmen's attention to it. Meanwhile, Carmen paced slowly around the room.

"Come on, show me one way or the other," she called out.

Tina knew it might be best to leave the house for a while. She seemed to be doing more harm than good. But maybe if Carmen noticed the Book of Mormon she would look through it.

With memories of pushing Frank's radio buttons fresh in her mind, Tina felt confident she could move the book. She went to the desk and gripped the book with both hands—being careful not to pass through it—hoping to nudge it ahead just enough that Carmen might see it.

Carmen turned toward the desk just as a blue book zoomed at her. It stopped abruptly three feet above the floor, then fell to the carpet at Carmen's feet. All Tina could do was wince, knowing she had really crossed the line this time.

Carmen's nerves snapped. She picked up the book and ripped all the pages from the spine. "You don't scare me," she whispered fiercely. Then she gathered up all the pages and carried them outside to the trash can.

Tina sadly followed behind her mother, knowing she had used her influence the wrong way. "What was I thinking?" she asked herself.

Suddenly Tina felt herself being pulled by a powerful force—as if the world's largest vacuum had sucked her up. She rocketed back through the veil and within moments she was back in her spirit world apartment, face-to-face with an angry Grandma Lucille.

"Oops," Tina said, trying to smile.

Lucille wasn't amused. "Tina, what did I tell you? Don't tamper with the physical world! You've been doing so well! What made you decide to move that book?"

Tina frowned. "It felt like a good idea to get her to read the Book of Mormon."

Lucille gave her a stern look. "I think Carmen will have a hard time reading a ripped-up book. Now Kim can't read it, either. The council members are not pleased . . ."

"What? This just happened! They know already?"

"Of course they know," Lucille said. "They could overlook you tampering with the car radio—that's a fairly common mistake—although your father wouldn't have been so distracted at work if you hadn't been fooling around. Since his injury might turn out to be a blessing in disguise in reuniting the family, the council agreed to overlook your first infraction. However, moving the Book of Mormon was too much."

Lucille paced around the room, then faced Tina. "I told you plainly that we can't interfere in the physical world! We have to use our feelings—spirit to spirit. When someone interferes like you just did, the council nearly always ends the assignment."

"I'm making progress," Tina said defensively. "Both Kim and Mom have sensed my presence."

"I know, but I'll bet the council is already assigning someone else to your family," Lucille said wearily. "I might regret this, but my son's eternal life is at stake. I'm going to ask the council to let you keep your assignment. Don't leave this room until I get back."

# CHAPTER NINETEEN

———— ❧ ————

Soon after Lucille's departure, Ida visited Tina. She'd heard about Tina's mistake, but she wasn't there to chastise her. Ida had hoped Tina would open a way for her into Paradise, but now things looked pretty bleak.

Tina had been feeling really low, so she was actually glad to have some company. "Grandma said I'll be replaced," Tina said. "Who would they send instead?"

Ida pondered for a moment. "Possibly your Aunt Evelyn, but she's only directly related to your father. She probably wouldn't have much effect on your sister or mother."

"Maybe they'll send you," Tina said.

"I doubt it," Ida said. "It seems that the more recently a spirit has lived on earth, the more effective they are in those kinds of assignments. I haven't been back to the mortal world since my burial, so I'd be useless. I've seen images of those automobiles and airplanes, but I'd feel out of place there. I'm not used to anything faster than a horse. In fact, I've probably regressed."

"Why do you say that?" Tina asked.

"Not long after I died and accepted the gospel, I was assigned to the far reaches of Spirit Prison to work with our ancestors who lived in Europe during the Dark Ages. They required a lot of patience, and they didn't really make much progress. Even teaching them how to be polite was a challenge."

Tina smiled. "The modern world has plenty of rude people, so maybe you're already qualified."

"No, you're the best one for the job," Ida said. "Let's hope the council realizes that."

Tina instinctively gave Ida a hug. "I'm so sorry," she said. "I know you were counting on me. If I get another chance, I won't let you down."

～

Lucille didn't return to the apartment for a long time. Tina and Ida weren't sure whether that was a good or bad sign. When Lucille finally rejoined them, she looked very solemn and collapsed onto the couch.

"After much debate, the council has decided to give you another chance," she said. "But you are on probation, so please be wise."

Ida gave Tina a nudge and said, "In other words, don't move things!"

Tina nodded with relief. She much preferred her current assignment over teaching people from the Dark Ages. The girls had a farewell hug, then Lucille escorted Tina back through the veil into a hazy January afternoon in Layton. There were two inches of snow on the ground. As they hovered above the Marlar home, Lucille apologized.

"I'm sorry I got angry," she said. "I just feel Frank might return to the Church, and I know the blessings it would bring your family. I want you all to be living in Paradise, including Ida, and you're really the only one who can influence your family right now."

"I know, Grandma," Tina said. "I'll be more careful."

Lucille then added, "Please be aware that two days have passed on earth since your mother tore up the Book of Mormon."

"Really? I'm still not accustomed to the way time zooms by," Tina said. "Is there anything else I should know?"

"Carmen hasn't mentioned the 'floating book' to anyone, but she's still shaken up about it. Kim has noticed her Book of Mormon is missing, but she doesn't want to say anything to your parents. She suspects your father took it, but she also knows he couldn't have made it up the stairs with his injured leg. So things are a bit unsettled. Just do your best and follow the promptings you will receive."

Tina nodded, then passed through the front door once again. Frank was watching TV on the couch. The clock showed 2:30. Kim was still at school, and since the car wasn't in the driveway, Carmen must have gone shopping.

Tina hovered next to her father, who was watching a talk show featuring two men who claimed to be the lost sons of Elvis Presley and wanted an inheritance.

"This world has problems," she said.

Frank's leg was propped up on the arm of the couch, and every few moments he tried to reach behind him. Tina noticed the TV remote control had fallen just out of his grasp. His anger seemed ready to boil over.

Tina moved to the window, watching for her mother to arrive. Just then, two men in white shirts walked past the house, and she felt prompted to go out to them. She zoomed out of the house and read their nametags. They were missionaries for the LDS Church!

"What could it hurt if they stopped by to visit Dad?" Tina asked herself. "It would sure be better than what he's doing right now. Maybe they'd even help him retrieve the remote control."

Tina moved in front of the missionaries and shouted, "Stop right there!"

One of the missionaries walked straight through her, but the other one, whose nametag read Elder Brown, acted as if he'd run into a brick wall. "Go knock on that door," Tina told him, then she stepped away.

Elder Brown called to his companion, "Hey, Elder Rhees! Come back. I think we need to visit this house."

Elder Rhees looked back skeptically. "It doesn't even look like anyone is home."

"Let's give it a try at least."

Elder Brown marched toward the door. His companion joined him, and they rang the doorbell. To their surprise, they heard someone yell, "Come in."

The missionaries peeked in the door and saw Frank resting on the couch.

"Hello, sir," Elder Brown said.

Frank looked up and groaned. "Oh, not you guys," he said tiredly. "I'm not interested."

Elder Brown wasn't about to be pushed aside that easily. "Sir, we were just walking through the neighborhood and felt we should knock on your door."

"Isn't that what you tell everybody?" Frank asked.

Elder Brown looked a little offended. "Not at all. I really think we're supposed to talk to you."

Frank didn't believe him, but said, "I'll tell you what. If you hand me the remote control, I'll listen for thirty seconds."

The missionaries hurried in and Elder Brown handed Frank the remote control.

"Well, I'll get started," he said quickly. "I'm guessing you aren't a member of the LDS Church?"

"That's right," Frank said. "I don't plan to be, either."

"What religion do you belong to?" Elder Brown asked.

"I'm not religious at all," Frank said. "However, I'm really bored. If you'd come last week during the college bowl games, I would've sent you on your way, but today I can either listen to you or watch another bad talk show. Look at those guys! If you shaved off their sideburns they wouldn't look a thing like Elvis."

Elder Brown grinned. "I'm glad we rate slightly better than daytime television."

"We'll see," Frank said, without a hint of humor. He pointed the remote control at the TV and turned down the volume, but he didn't turn it off.

Elder Brown nodded toward Frank's propped-up leg. "What happened?"

Frank shook his head in disgust. "I got a little careless and burned myself at work."

"Where do you work?" Elder Brown asked.

"I'm a mechanic at Hill Air Force Base," Frank said. "I work on the bigger planes. Anyway, I'm out of commission for a while, so entertain me. Tell me about yourselves."

"I'm Elder Brown, from Irvine, California, and this is my companion Elder Rhees."

Elder Rhees briefly nodded at Frank, but he was also keeping an eye on the TV. Frank wasn't impressed at all by the younger missionary—but he admired Elder Brown's confidence.

"You're from California, and you got to travel all the way to Utah?" Frank asked. "What a rotten deal! I would've asked for a new assignment."

"I really like it here," Elder Brown said. "My sister Becky is serving a mission in the Canary Islands right now, and I don't think I'd trade places with her. I've had more baptisms than she has."

Frank laughed. "Really? You guys actually baptize people here? I thought people in Utah were either already members, or they felt like I do—'No way!'"

"You'd be surprised," Elder Brown said. He stood to look at a framed photo on the far wall. It showed two smiling teenage girls wearing Mickey Mouse ears.

"Are these your daughters?" Elder Brown asked. "They look familiar to me."

"I doubt you know them," Frank said. "Kim, my older daughter, is a senior at Layton High. And Tina, she's … uh, she died not too long ago."

Elder Brown snapped around with true concern in his eyes. "I'm so sorry to hear that. Tina has a glow about her."

Frank shifted on the couch and suddenly cleared his throat. "Well, thanks for grabbing the remote control for me, but I'm not interested in your church. If you don't mind, I think I'll stick to daytime TV."

He turned up the volume louder than it was before, snapping Elder Rhees out of his daze. Elder Brown tried to salvage the visit by asking, "Could we leave you a pamphlet or maybe a Book of Mormon to read?"

One look into Frank's sad, angry eyes let Elder Brown know

he'd touched a sensitive nerve. He was glad Frank wasn't able to get off the couch.

"Well, Elder Rhees, I think we better go," Elder Brown said with forced cheerfulness. Elder Rhees was already halfway to the door.

Frank regained his composure. "I didn't mean to be rude, but Tina's death has hit me hard. It's the last thing I want to talk about today."

"That's fine," Elder Brown said, approaching Frank and shaking his hand. "Sorry to have bothered you."

Tina had watched the whole episode while standing behind her father. She first felt excitement, but then disappointment came as her father acted just as she might have expected. However, an idea came to her as the missionaries closed the door. She followed Elder Brown and shouted over and over, "Leave a Book of Mormon on the porch!"

Elder Brown stopped on the porch, opened his backpack, and pulled out a copy of the Book of Mormon. He quickly wrote inside the front cover, "We are Elder Brown and Elder Rhees. We'd like to talk to you about the LDS Church." Then he added the phone number and propped it against the door.

"Why are you wasting time on that guy?" Elder Rhees asked. "He's not golden."

Elder Brown shrugged and asked, "What can it hurt?" Then the missionaries continued down the road.

Tina clapped her hands. It had worked! Elder Brown seemed more responsive to her influences than any mortal she'd ever met. Now Tina offered a heartfelt prayer that Kim would get home before Carmen did. Things could get pretty interesting if Carmen discovered the book.

Then to Tina's horror a large dog came wandering across the lawn and onto the porch. Tina tried to kick him away, but her leg went right through him. The dog stopped to sniff the book, and Tina was frantic. She wasn't going to let this dog ruin everything that had just occurred. She mustered all her energy and shouted,

"Get out of here, you ugly mutt!"

The dog's ears immediately shot up, then it scampered away in fear. Tina stayed right on the dog's tail, shouting at the animal until it was several houses away. She smiled as the frightened dog caught up to the missionaries and sent Elder Rhees scampering into the street.

Then to Tina's delight, Kim walked around the corner coming from the opposite direction. She waved at Elder Brown, who despite being a great missionary, couldn't resist taking a peek back at her after she had passed. The missionaries turned at the next corner, and Tina hurried back to the porch.

Kim almost didn't notice the book, then she reached down and grabbed it in surprise. She opened the cover and read Elder Brown's words, looked nervously around, then slipped it into her purse before entering the house. She happily greeted Frank and told him all about her day—except the part about finding a Book of Mormon on the porch.

❦

Before going to bed, Kim shut her bedroom door and quietly dialed the number written in the front of the Book of Mormon. After two rings Kim heard, "Hello, this is Elder Brown. May I help you?"

"Uh, yes, hello," Kim sputtered. "I found a Book of Mormon on my porch today, and felt I should give you a call."

"Hmm. I left books on two porches today," Elder Brown said. "You don't sound like the grumpy guy with the burned leg, and you certainly aren't the old toothless lady who fed us some stale cookies. I'll never forget that voice."

Kim smiled. "I'm Kim Marlar, the daughter of the grumpy guy with the burned leg. Actually, I think I waved to you guys today. Were you the missionary on the sidewalk, or the one being chased by a dog?"

"That was me on the sidewalk," Elder Brown said with a laugh.

"How can I help you? Don't tell me—your father wants us to come back tomorrow."

"Hardly," Kim said. "I'm just calling to find out how you knew I'd lost my Book of Mormon."

Elder Brown paused. "I . . . I didn't. I just felt I should leave the book."

"Well, I'm glad you did," Kim said. "I'm very interested, but I have a few obstacles . . ."

"I think we met your biggest obstacle," Elder Brown said.

"Yes, Dad is causing me some problems," Kim said. "My mom isn't much better. Any suggestions?"

"Kim, how old are you?" Elder Brown asked.

"Seventeen, but I turn eighteen next month."

"We don't want to go against your parents' wishes, and until you're eighteen there's not much we can do without their consent," Elder Brown said. "I'll tell you what. We'll slip some pamphlets under your doormat tomorrow. Spend the next month reading them and the Book of Mormon, and then give us a call when you turn eighteen—or sooner if your dad changes his mind."

"Okay, that will be good," Kim said. "I'll talk to Dad and see what he says . . ."

"We'll plan on talking to you in a month," Elder Brown said with a chuckle.

# CHAPTER TWENTY

Kim waited nervously at a corner table in Layton's Sizzler Restaurant as her parents returned from the salad bar. Frank's leg was slowly healing, and now he was able to hobble around a bit on his own.

It was February 11th, Kim's eighteenth birthday, and her parents had surprised her with an impromptu dinner. She was about to surprise them, too. In the past month she had secretly finished reading the Book of Mormon that Elder Brown had left on their porch.

After finishing the book, Kim didn't receive a firm answer whether it was true when she prayed about it. She'd been frustrated, but she continued to pray about it, and one night while praying a strong feeling rushed through her, bringing her to tears. She knew it was the confirmation she had sought. She also knew the messages were true she had read in the pamphlets about Joseph Smith and the restoration of the Church of Jesus Christ.

As her parents settled into their chairs, Kim hesitated to say anything. Her mother had been acting strangely for nearly a month, and finally last week she had told Kim and Frank about the flying Book of Mormon. Carmen's strange story had briefly disturbed Kim, but she figured it must have been an evil spirit trying to destroy the book. It had been a relief to know where her original book had ended up, though.

Kim waited until the waitress brought their meals, then she put on a bright smile and said, "Thanks so much for the birthday dinner. It means a lot to me."

Her parents smiled back. "Well, it has been a difficult few months, but you've been such a strength to us," Frank said.

Kim kept that smile frozen on her face as she said, "I just want you to know that now that I'm eighteen I'll be joining the LDS Church as soon as I can."

Her parents' smiles vanished. Carmen slowly placed her fork down on the table, and a steely look came into her eyes.

"I don't believe what I'm hearing," she said. "Didn't I explain clearly enough that I saw a Book of Mormon flying through the air? I thought it was going to attack me!"

"Mom, I can't explain why that happened, but even if you did see a flying book, it was my book! You had no right to tear it up!"

"It was possessed, Kim. I had to destroy it."

The family at the next table suddenly went silent, and two teenagers peered over at the Marlars. Kim ignored their glances.

"This has nothing to do with the book," she said. "This is about letting me make my own choices, and you two aren't willing to do that. What does it take? I'm a good person, yet I sometimes feel I'll never measure up. Do I have to die like Tina did?"

Both tables were now silent. Finally Carmen stood and grabbed her purse. "I've lost my appetite," she said. "Let's go."

She left some money on the table to pay for the tip, then stalked off to the car.

Despite her outburst, Kim still helped Frank hobble back to the car. Carmen already had the engine running, and they were silent on the way home. Frank turned the radio to a Utah Jazz basketball game and the tension momentarily ebbed, but as soon as they walked in the front door Kim asked her father, "I know you don't like the Mormons, but don't you believe in God or Jesus?"

Frank shrugged uncomfortably. "I suppose."

"Then that means you believe the Bible," Kim said. "Stay right there."

She ran to her school bookbag and pulled out a pamphlet the missionaries had put under the doormat. The pamphlet talked about some of the early converts to the LDS Church who had left their families in Europe to be with the Saints in America. Kim understood how they felt, and she had been waiting for the right moment to quote a certain scripture to her parents. The time had come.

Kim stood in front of her parents and said, "This is what Jesus told people who felt they couldn't give up worldly things for spiritual things." She paused and found the spot in the pamphlet. "'And every one that hath forsaken houses, or brethren, or sisters, or father, or mother, or wife, or children, or lands, for my name's sake, shall receive an hundredfold, and shall inherit everlasting life.' That's what I'll do if you don't support my decision to be baptized."

Her parents were stunned by her words. Frank just shook his head. "Kim, don't be foolish. We only want the best for you. The Mormons are leading you down the wrong path."

Kim's eyes flashed. "You really think so? You both know Nicole. She doesn't swear, smoke, drink, or stay out late with boys. You're saying that you would prefer I do those things?"

Frank forced a smile. "Of course not. Nicole is very nice, but she's a rare one …"

Kim waved her hand to cut him off. "That's a lie. There are hundreds of LDS kids like her at my school."

Carmen tried to intervene. "Kim, let's sleep on this. You're acting a little crazy."

"Crazy?" she asked in despair. "All I want is to be with Tina again someday, and I'll never make it to heaven living in this house."

Kim stomped past Frank and marched back out the door. Carmen and Frank looked at each other, realizing if they didn't act quickly they'd lose another daughter. Carmen caught up with Kim on the sidewalk. She grabbed her daughter's arm and said, "Don't break our family apart."

"I don't understand you two," Kim cried. "All I want to do is become closer to God and be a better person, and you're acting like it's the end of the world!"

Carmen looked at the ground, realizing her daughter felt betrayed by the people she loved the most.

"Let's just forget about the flying Book of Mormon . . . and forsaking your parents," Carmen said. "At this point, I want to do whatever makes you happy. I just want the fighting to stop. As for your father . . ."

Carmen glanced back at the house where Frank was listening on the porch. Kim's eyes narrowed. "What has Dad said?"

Carmen looked back intently. "You know Dad hates the Mormons, but he would prefer you joining them than to have you leave us."

Kim shook her head. "That's not enough. I've learned I could do a baptism in the temple for Tina, and I want to do that for her."

"I can't let that happen," Frank called out.

"Why do you care so much about it?" Kim shouted tearfully. "If the LDS Church is false, then what does it matter? But if it's true, think what it will mean to Tina!"

Carmen lowered her voice to a whisper. "Right now let's take it one step at a time. Once you're baptized, then we'll see what happens with the temple stuff."

"But Mom—"

"Several little steps will still get you where you want to go," Carmen said cautiously. "But two big steps right now will really hurt your father."

Kim stared at the ground for nearly a minute, then finally nodded. She walked back to the house and passed Frank without saying a word. She went straight to the phone and dialed the number she had memorized. After a pause, she said, "Elder Brown? This is Kim Marlar. I turned eighteen today, and I'm ready to take the missionary lessons."

At Kim's side stood a very relieved Tina. She had nervously watched the evening's outbursts, knowing the day would be a turning point for her family. Thankfully Kim had stood firm, and Carmen had become a peacemaker. The "flying Book of Mormon" had caused some major problems, but now things appeared to be back on track.

# CHAPTER TWENTY-ONE

Once Kim got off the phone, Frank had only one request. "The missionary discussions have to be taught here," Frank told Kim. "Also, your mother has to be in attendance."

"What about you?" Carmen and Kim asked in unison.

Frank shrugged. "We'll see, but don't count on it." Then he gave a slight grin to Carmen. "Maybe I need to be there. That one guy—I think his name is Elder Brown—is pretty charismatic. He's not ugly, either. We don't need Kim running off with him."

"Daddy! Don't be ridiculous," Kim said. She had only seen Elder Brown the time she had waved to him on the sidewalk, but she had really liked his personality on the phone.

The next night at 7 p.m. the missionaries rang the doorbell, and Frank answered the door. Elder Brown introduced his new companion, Elder Williams, and then the missionaries shook hands with Carmen and Kim.

"What happened to that other guy?" Frank asked.

"He got transferred to Ogden," Elder Brown said.

"I'm glad he's gone," Frank said. "I've never seen anyone so glued to a TV in all my life."

Frank excused himself and went upstairs. The others settled into the living room, where Tina waited eagerly for the discussion to begin. Suddenly Ruby, her nemesis from the Spirit World, entered the room.

"Hey, what are you doing here?" Tina demanded, grabbing her meddling relative by the shoulder.

"There must be opposition in all things," Ruby said with a

sneer. "It's right there in the scriptures. I'm here to make sure both sides get a fair shake."

Tina couldn't believe it. "Don't you think your side has enough going for it?" she asked. "Teenage girls hardly have a chance! Isn't immodesty, suggestive music, parties, and alcohol enough?"

"It's never enough," Ruby said with a wicked grin. "Besides, all is fair in love and war, and this is war! Do you realize the problems Kim will cause if she joins the LDS Church? She could lead entire generations straight into Paradise! I won't even get a shot at them on the other side. I can't let that happen."

Elder Brown began talking about Joseph Smith, and Ruby immediately dashed to Kim's side. "Lies! Lies! All of it is lies! Joseph Smith is a fraud," Ruby shouted. "Life ends at death! The Savior can't save you!"

Tina was stunned by Ruby's ferocity. Although she'd never been much of a fighter, the time had come. Tina lowered her shoulder and barreled into Ruby, sending her sprawling through Elder Brown. Ruby hopped up and came back at her, but Tina grabbed Ruby's hair and yanked down hard, causing Ruby to nosedive through the floor. Tina then jumped on Ruby's back and pounded the back of her head.

"Get off me!" Ruby screamed. "That's not fair! You're not letting me do my job!"

Meanwhile, the discussion was going smoothly—until Ruby bucked Tina off her back and right through Carmen, who suddenly shook her head as if dizzy. Then the two spirits converged in front of Kim, where a classic catfight ensued. As spirits, Ruby and Tina couldn't actually hurt each other, but they were causing a major commotion nonetheless.

In one dimension a peaceful, spiritual discussion was taking place, while in the exact same spot two very feisty women were fighting like demons—well, Ruby technically *was* a demon. Finally the pair's biting, clawing, and shrieking began to affect the mortal world.

Kim stopped Elder Brown. "I'm feeling confused," she said.

"Something doesn't feel right."

Elder Brown nodded. "You know what? We forgot to begin our discussion with a prayer. Would it be all right if Elder Williams offered one for us?"

At those words, Ruby froze. "Uh oh," she whispered.

In Elder Williams' prayer he asked that Kim would understand the lesson, and then he said, "At this time, we also ask for special protection over this house from the adversary, so that this discussion might go forward in peace."

Almost instantly a large white-robed spirit swooped in through the ceiling. He looked similar to the warrior spirits Tina had seen at the Bountiful Temple. Ruby's eyes widened. She quickly let go of Tina and shouted, "I'll get even with you later."

Ruby then vanished through the wall. The warrior turned toward Tina, who cried out, "Hey, I'm on your side!"

"I know," he said with a smile. "You did a great job. I think you could've handled her."

"You were watching?" Tina asked.

"Yes, but I couldn't step in until someone asked for help," he said. "I was glad when the missionaries finally got on the ball. You shouldn't hesitate to ask for help next time, either."

The warrior waved good-bye and said, "I'll make sure Ruby gets back to Spirit Prison where she belongs."

He then rose through the ceiling, and Tina gave a sigh of relief as she settled onto the couch next to her sister. Kim's eyes were sparkling at the words of the missionaries, and Tina smiled, knowing her sister would soon join the Lord's kingdom!

# CHAPTER TWENTY-TWO

Tina was now spending each night outside the Bountiful Temple, anticipating the day she could enter inside. She visited with Aaron when he had some free time, and they were becoming good friends. But on the night after battling Ruby, Tina received a special visit at the temple from Lucille.

"You did well," Lucille told her. "Ruby was affecting the spirituality in the room, and you were wise to battle her. But just say a prayer for help next time."

"I will," Tina said. "I don't want to fight Ruby again. She's like a wild animal."

"I truly pity her," Lucille said. "She was born into the Church, but she has turned against goodness in every way. She has actually gotten worse in the Spirit World. She tries to disrupt any spiritual progress our family members make. Her goal is for everyone to be as miserable as she is."

Tina couldn't help feeling sad for Ruby. "She appeared in my room a few days before I died," Tina said. "What was she doing?"

"She's been trying to tempt you and Kim for years. Since you two weren't members of the Church on earth, you seemed like easy targets. She's furious that you won't be joining her side."

"I had a bad feeling about Ruby the moment I met her on the plaza in the Spirit World," Tina said. "Don't worry, I'll be on guard for any other tricks she might be planning."

The missionaries taught Kim another discussion two days later. Tina also attended this discussion and was happy that her mother seemed to be soaking it all in. Frank had decided to skip this discussion too, choosing to watch a Jazz game. On the other hand, Nicole had come to participate, and the missionaries were glad to see her. Who wouldn't prefer having another cute teenage girl join the group instead of having to deal with Frank?

As the second discussion ended, Elder Brown asked, "Kim, are you willing to be baptized?"

Kim rolled her eyes. "Of course. That's why we're here, isn't it?"

The group laughed. Elder Brown said, "You're right, and the next step is to attend church. Will you be able to attend our meetings on Sunday?"

For some reason, Kim hadn't really thought much about that. She'd never attended a church service of any kind. But Nicole perked up and said, "I'll stop by at 10:45 on Sunday morning, and we can walk there together. You'll really like it."

Kim turned to Carmen. "Will that be all right?"

Carmen smiled. "I don't think I could stop you if I tried."

"Great," Elder Brown said. "We'll see you there."

☙

As Kim entered the church that Sunday, she realized the missionaries and Nicole's family must've given the church members advance notice, because she could hardly walk five feet without people introducing themselves and shaking her hand. However, she admittedly liked all of the attention. Kim met Bishop Reynolds, and she immediately felt good about him. She sensed he was a gentle, caring man who was truly pleased she had chosen to be baptized.

The meetings seemed to pass slowly, but as Kim walked home with Nicole, she had the same feeling in her heart she'd felt that night while praying about the Book of Mormon. It was true!

If only Kim could have seen her proud little sister walking on the other side of her. Tina could hardly contain her excitement, and she did a few backflips in the air to show her joy.

❧

Two weeks later, on the first Saturday of March, a standing-room-only crowd gathered to witness Kim's baptism. Tina had arrived early at the church, making sure she didn't have to prompt the missionaries in case they'd forgotten to fill the baptismal font, but everything was in perfect order.

Tina watched Kim come into the room, radiantly clothed in a white dress. Elder Brown also entered the room dressed in white. Kim had asked him to baptize her, and Tina couldn't help noticing the growing affection between them.

Carmen sat next to Kim on the front row and was busy meeting all of Kim's new friends as they passed by to congratulate her. Bishop Reynolds was especially attentive to Carmen and made her feel very welcome. Tina was disappointed Frank had begged off coming, claiming his leg was acting up, but Kim had taken it well. Carmen had take a photo of Kim and Frank together before leaving home, and they had departed on happy terms.

The baptismal service began with a song and prayer, then Nicole stood before the group to give a short message. She wisely realized she was addressing Carmen as much as she was Kim.

She gave them both a nervous smile, then said, "In the Book of Mormon, the prophet Nephi compares baptism to a gate leading to heaven. Picture in your mind that Heavenly Father lives in a beautiful white home that is surrounded by a tall white fence. The fence has only one opening—a sparkling gate that lets us enter the path to the home.

"If we never enter the gate, we won't be able to live with our Heavenly Father. But today Kim is entering that gate, and as she keeps the commandments and stays on the right path, at the end of her life she will find herself at the door to that beautiful white home, and Heavenly Father will welcome her in!"

Nicole paused to brush away a tear. "Jesus set the example for us by being baptized, and I know He is happy Kim is following his example today. Thank you, Kim, for being such a good friend and example to me. I'm so happy you're becoming a member of the Church."

As Nicole closed her talk and returned to her seat, Carmen reached out and briefly clutched Nicole's hand. "Thank you so much," Carmen told her.

Carmen then turned to Kim and whispered, "I wish your father could have heard that."

Then Elder Brown led Kim down into the water. Tina stood next to her mother to watch the baptism. Kim seemed completely at peace, but Elder Brown seemed very nervous. He took Kim by the wrist, then raised his right arm and said, "Kimberly Marlar, having been commissioned of Jesus Christ, I baptize you in the name of the Father, and of the Son, and of the Holy Ghost. Amen."

He then carefully lowered her backward into the water and pushed her nearly to the bottom of the font, carefully watching to make sure every inch of Kim had been submerged. He glanced at the two men standing at the edge of the font who were acting as witnesses, and seeing their approving nods, he pulled her quickly from the water. To his surprise, Kim came up right into his arms and gave him a tight squeeze before moving up the font's stairs and toward the dressing room.

"Elder, watch yourself," Elder Williams said good-naturedly, and the crowd laughed.

Kim poked her head back into the font and smilingly told the crowd, "What's wrong? I'm happy!" This sent another ripple of laughter through the group.

Tina looked around the room at the happy faces, and was surprised to see her grandparents, Lucille and Samuel, standing near the back of the room. She floated over to them and gave them a hug.

"I didn't know you were here," she said. "Why didn't you signal to me?"

Lucille smiled. "You looked so content watching your sister. We didn't want to disturb you."

Samuel had a big grin. "This is a great day for us, too," he said. "We have prayed for many years that you and Kim would find the gospel. We wouldn't miss this moment for anything."

As wonderful as the baptism was, Kim's confirmation as a member of the Church was even more powerful for Tina. After emerging from the dressing room in a beautiful new dress, Kim settled into a chair in the front of the room.

A group of priesthood holders gathered around her and placed their hands on her head. Grandpa Samuel also moved forward and melded into the circle next to Elder Williams, who began by confirming Kim a member of the Church of Jesus Christ of Latter-day Saints and bestowing upon her the gift of the Holy Ghost.

Elder Williams paused, and Tina noticed Grandpa Samuel whispering into the missionary's ear. Elder Williams then said, "Kim, you have a special role in your family. Your mission in life is to unite those here on earth with those who have accepted the gospel in the Spirit World. I bless you with the ability to be the link between this world and the next. Seek out your ancestors, and most importantly, prepare the way for your sister Tina to enter Paradise."

Elder Williams ended the blessing and then stepped away from the circle. There wasn't a dry eye in the room. Elder Williams was in a state of shock. He told Kim, "You've mentioned you had a sister pass away, but I didn't know her name was Tina. I don't know where those words came from."

"I do," Kim said with joyful tears streaming down her cheeks. "My sister is ready to join the Church, too."

# CHAPTER TWENTY-THREE

Kim tried to downplay the events of the day as she and Carmen ate dinner with Frank that night, but Carmen had been spiritually touched at the baptismal service and she kept describing parts of it to Frank.

"Enough already," Frank said half-jokingly. "See, Kim? I didn't need to go. Your mother has told me everything."

"Well, not everything," Carmen said. "When the missionary gave Kim the ghost power—"

"The gift of the Holy Ghost, Mom," Kim politely corrected.

"Oh, yes," Carmen said with a smile. "Anyway, he blessed her that she could help Tina get into Paradise, even though he'd never heard Tina's name before."

Frank looked surprised. "He actually said that?"

"I don't recall mentioning Tina, other than saying 'my sister' a couple of times during the discussion about the Plan of Salvation," Kim said. "That's what makes it so strange."

Frank stayed quiet. Then Kim softly said, "Dad, I would like to go to the temple and be baptized for Tina."

Tina had been with them throughout the day, and she now nervously watched her father. Could it actually happen?

Frank slowly chewed on a piece of steak, then glanced at Carmen. "It's your decision," he said to his wife, then he put another bite into his mouth.

Carmen and Kim smiled at each other, knowing what a monstrous obstacle had just been overcome. Kim felt like squealing in delight, but she calmly asked Carmen, "Mom, is it okay if I get

Tina's temple work done? I'll take care of everything."

Carmen winked at her daughter. "That would be fine."

Kim smiled as the family quietly continued eating, but Tina felt a surge of joy and couldn't contain herself. She jumped around the kitchen, bouncing off the fridge and stove before literally dancing on the ceiling. "Yes!" she shouted. "I'm going to Paradise!"

❧

Kim had done her best during the meal at hiding her excitement from Frank, but she slipped upstairs and searched the phone book for their local Family History Center. She called and discovered it was open until 9 p.m. that night. Once her parents were settled watching TV, Kim told them she was going out for a while.

Kim drove to the center with Tina riding along. "I know you can't hear me," Tina told her, "but thank you so much for doing what is right. I love you!"

Tina stayed by her sister's side as Kim nervously walked into the building. She was greeted by a kindly man who wore a badge that read Elder Lewis.

"Hello," he said. "How can I help you tonight?"

"Well, I got baptized today, and my parents have agreed I can now do the temple work for my younger sister who passed away."

"That's wonderful," Elder Lewis said. "I can certainly help you with that."

He led her to a computer and opened the FamilySearch webpage and helped her open an account. Under his guidance, Kim found her Marlar grandparents' records and added her parents' information. She then typed in Tina's birth information before coming to the line for her death date. Kim said, "Tina died on the sixth of September."

For the first time, Elder Lewis frowned. "Hmmm," he said. "It's not a big problem, but the Church requires we wait a full year after a person's death before doing any temple work for them."

"But why?" Kim asked in alarm. "I know in my heart that Tina has accepted the gospel and is eager to join the Church."

"That's right," Tina said anxiously to their unhearing ears.

Elder Lewis looked a bit apprehensive, but said, "I'm afraid we can't bend the rules. It applies throughout the Church. The system simply won't let you proceed until a year has passed. But on September 6th you can print your sister's card and take it to the temple to do the work."

Kim asked a few more questions, but she quickly saw there weren't any other options. Two disappointed Marlar girls left the building. Tina moved close to Kim and said, "Thank you. I can certainly wait."

At that moment Tina felt a comforting presence next to her, and Grandma Lucille appeared. "I can't be baptized yet," Tina told her sadly.

"I know, but don't be upset," Lucille said. "You're on your way! Just think of poor Ida."

Lucille took Tina by the arm. "I've come to take you back to the Spirit World," she said. "We can use your help. Kim's baptism has opened up a whole new opportunity for you."

They paused to watch Kim get into the car. "She's doing so well," Lucille said happily. "She'll be fine without you for a while."

# Chapter Twenty-Four

Lucille and Tina popped back into the Spirit World and returned to the Marlar apartment complex. "We'll only be here for a little while," Lucille said. "I just need to show you some more details about your mother's family."

Tina remembered the scenes she had seen in the Learning Center. She knew her mother was from Peru, and she had seen images of an older couple. She also recalled being descended from the Incas.

As the screen in the wall of her apartment flickered to life, Tina found herself in a dense jungle. Nearby she saw a young olive-skinned couple holding an infant. She realized these people were her ancestors. Tina watched that baby grow into a man named Nimhi. He became a great leader among the Inca people just before the arrival of the Spaniards in the early 1500s.

The scene changed and Tina saw Nimhi taken captive and betrayed by the Spaniards. Most of his family members were killed. A few of Tina's ancestors managed to escape deep into the mountainous jungle, and for many generations they were isolated from any other people.

Carmen's parents were among the first to come down from the mountains, and they were the first to have a chance to hear the gospel. They knew of "Los Mormones" in the white shirts and ties, but had never really spoken to them. Frank's decision not to serve a mission had delayed everything.

Tina turned to Lucille. "I know my father's choices caused a lot of problems, but how can I help? I'm not even baptized yet myself."

"That's true, but you know the gospel teachings," Lucille said. "You're the first one in your mother's family to fully understand the gospel. The governing council has asked that you live among your ancestors and teach them. If Kim stays on track, the way will soon open up for your ancestors to enter into Paradise. However, they have to be taught the gospel first, and they haven't even been exposed to it. In fact, they hardly know what has gone on in the mortal world for the past 500 years. Of course, every family member that arrives in the Spirit World gives them an update of earth life, but they have all lived in that same part of Peru. For starters, you might give them a world history lesson."

Tina was overwhelmed. "I don't know if I can do that."

Lucille just smiled. "You know the gospel very well, and anything you tell them will be welcomed eagerly. Your ancestors will be very excited to see you. Are you ready?"

Tina shrugged. "I guess so."

They left the apartment and traveled quickly in a completely new direction over hundreds of beautiful communities, all perfectly aligned. This pattern of cities seemed to stretch out endlessly. Tina and Lucille zoomed across the landscape for thousands of miles and still hadn't reached their destination.

"I can't believe how big the Spirit World is," Tina said. "Does it ever end?"

"Yes, it has boundaries, but the Lord planned ahead and made it very large, knowing millions of spirits would eventually live here."

Finally in the distance a towering peak jutted into the sky. "We're nearly there," Lucille said. They slowed down above a city built on the foothills of the great mountain.

"This area feels just as I imagine Peru would," Tina said.

The buildings reminded Tina of the decaying Inca temples she had seen in a history book, except these buildings sparkled, as if they'd been completed that day.

The pair's appearance in the sky had attracted the attention of some of the people in the city. These people pointed at them and called out to their neighbors. Tina noticed everyone wore brown robes—none of the robes were white like the ones Lucille and Tina were wearing. As they floated to the ground, dozens of spirits surrounded them. Lucille raised her hands, and the group quieted.

"We are here to see Nimhi," Lucille said. "Please let him know he has special  visitors bringing him light and truth."

The crowd whispered to each other, then a young man ran up the slope to the largest temple. Soon a man in a brightly colored robe came sweeping down the hillside, with several servants following him.

"Just follow my lead," Lucille whispered to Tina. Lucille then moved forward and bowed before the approaching group. Tina did the same, and within moments the man known as Nimhi stood before them.

"Arise and state your business," he said. He looked carefully at their radiant white robes and sensed these weren't typical messengers.

Lucille bowed slightly again. "I have come from Paradise, the land beyond the Great Gulf where the truths of the universe are found."

"We have heard of such a place," Nimhi said, "but we haven't dared journey beyond the horizon."

"Paradise does exist," Lucille said. "It is filled with glory, and it is possible for you to live there."

A stir passed through the group, especially when Lucille said, "My companion, Tina, is your descendant. She has the answers you have been looking for all of these years. She would like to live among you and teach you the eternal truths that will allow all of you to live forever with the Great Maker."

Nimhi's face filled with happiness. He stepped forward and took Tina by the hand. "It would be an honor to learn from you," he said. "Please teach these truths to me and my leaders, so we can share them with all of our people."

Tina gulped, feeling unqualified for the task, but she said, "As you wish."

Lucille winked at her and said, "I'll be back for you when your baptismal date arrives." Tina watched nervously as Lucille elevated above the crowd and waved good-bye. But Tina quickly forgot anything else as the people of the city surrounded her and led her to the Inca temple at the base of the towering mountain. She felt at peace. These people were refined and respectful—and most importantly, they were her family!

# CHAPTER TWENTY-FIVE

A week after Kim's baptism, Frank received a shocking phone call from his supervisor. He was being transferred. It would take months for his leg to get back to normal, so climbing around on airplanes was no longer an option. The personnel department had been watching for a suitable position for him, and one did open up—nearly a thousand miles away. Frank's new assignment was at Offutt Air Force Base near Omaha, Nebraska.

He first broke the news to Carmen. "They really need somebody to catalog the spare parts they've got stored there. With my injury, my superiors thought this would be best."

Carmen hung her head. "Frank, this is going to be hard. Kim's a senior in high school, and Tina's buried here—"

Frank cut in, "I don't have a choice."

Carmen knew this, but she scrambled for options. For a moment she considered that she and Kim could stay in Utah for a few months, but she quickly dismissed the idea. She and Frank needed to be together if their marriage was going to last.

"It looks like we're on our way to Nebraska," she finally said.

They anxiously waited for Kim to come home. When she walked through the door after school, she found both parents expectantly sitting on the couch.

"Honey, come sit down with us," Frank said. Kim immediately knew what was going on. Her father didn't realize it, but the only time he'd called her "Honey" throughout her life was when he was going to announce a transfer to a new city.

Kim's heart sank. "Where are we going this time?"

Frank tried to act pleased. "We aren't going too far. I'm being transferred to Nebraska."

To Kim, it wasn't close enough. It might as well have been Africa. "When are you supposed to be there?" Kim asked.

"They've given me two weeks."

"Okay," she said woodenly. "I think I'll go break the news to Nicole."

Kim felt her world was being ripped apart, and she needed to talk to someone other than her parents. She kept her emotions in check until she reached Nicole's house, but then the tears just started flowing as she told Nicole the whole situation.

"It's never been easy to move, but in the past I always had Tina with me," she cried. "Plus, I've never had a friend like you that I had to leave behind."

Nicole smiled through her own tears. "Thank you. I feel the same way about you. Isn't there a way you could stay here for the rest of the school year? We've got less than three months left. Then who knows? It looks like I'll be accepted to BYU, and you could be my roommate in Provo."

"That might work," Kim said, brightening a little. "I doubt I could get into BYU, but I could find a job down there."

"That sounds like a plan," Nicole said. "Hey, I'm sure my parents would let you stay here a few weeks."

"This is sounding good," Kim said. "Of course, I need to talk to my parents about it."

"And pray about it," Nicole added.

"I'll certainly do that, but I think I know what the answer will be."

Kim soon returned home and shared her plans with her parents. She was surprised by their disappointed expressions.

"What's wrong?" Kim asked. "You two wouldn't have to worry about me, and I could stay close with Nicole."

"Is this what you want?" Carmen asked.

"It really is. I love you both, but maybe this arrangement would be best for all of us."

"We'd love to have you come with us," Frank said. "All I ask is that you think it over a few days before making a final decision."

"I'll do that," Kim said. She gave each parent a hug, but in her mind, the decision was already made.

By Saturday, everything had been worked out. Nicole's parents were happy to let Kim stay with them through the summer. They had a spare bedroom, and Kim and Nicole spent most of the day getting the room ready for Kim to move in.

Carmen and Frank kept telling each other Kim was going to be moving out soon anyway, so it might as well be a situation where they knew where she would be staying. They admitted Nicole's parents were being more than generous.

❧

At church the next day, Bishop Reynolds announced that everyone between the ages of 14 and 18 would be meeting together for a special lesson during Sunday School. Kim and Nicole settled into their seats, wondering what could be so important.

The bishop stood before the group and said, "Last night I felt compelled that I should speak to you about patriarchal blessings. As your bishop, that's an area I haven't focused on like I should have. Please raise your hand if you have received your patriarchal blessing."

Nicole was one of only six people to raise their hands.

"That's about what I estimated, and we need to get on this immediately," the bishop said. "A patriarchal blessing is a wonderful opportunity for the Lord to share what your future holds."

The bishop spent the next several minutes talking about what a patriarchal blessing was. Most of it skipped over Kim's head, but she latched onto one phrase. The bishop had said the blessing would "help a person gain direction at key points in life." She was certainly at that stage.

At the end of the lesson, Bishop Reynolds said, "I've discussed this matter with our stake patriarch, Brother Cope, and he's willing to arrange for two blessings each Sunday evening for the next few weeks. I feel we should start with the oldest youth first. Do we have any 18-year-olds here who would like to receive a patriarchal blessing?"

Kim raised her hand, along with a boy in the back of the room. "Good," the bishop said. "Would you two be willing to meet with the patriarch next Sunday evening?"

Kim nodded, and a warm feeling filled her body. She knew this was right!

# Chapter Twenty-Six

Kim didn't tell her parents about the upcoming patriarchal blessing. The week was already busy enough. Frank spent a lot of time on the phone making sure they had an apartment to move into, plus he was trying to get the house in Layton on the market. Once it sold, they would buy a house in Nebraska.

On top of that, it was a hectic week spent mostly in packing boxes—and the difficult decision of what to keep of Tina's possessions. In the end, they put all of her stuff into three big boxes that Kim would keep with her at Nicole's house.

Frank and Carmen spent Sunday loading the moving van. They planned to roll out of town on Monday morning and reach Nebraska in time to get into their apartment before Frank had to start work on Thursday.

Kim helped all she could, except for a break to attend church. She felt slightly guilty about not traveling to Nebraska to help her parents unpack, but they hadn't even asked her to do so. Besides, her parents' apartment was in a complex where a lot of military families lived. They hoped there would be plenty of willing hands to help unpack the van.

When Sunday evening arrived, Kim had been fasting for 24 hours in preparation for her blessing. Her parents had been so frazzled with last-minute details they didn't even notice she hadn't eaten. She finally told her parents she had a short church meeting to attend.

"You already went to church today," Frank said. "Couldn't you stay and help us finish packing?"

"This will only take a few minutes," Kim said. "Then I'll be right back to help."

Frank grumbled a little, but then said, "Fine. Just hurry back."

The blessing would take place at Brother Cope's house. Kim didn't know where he lived, but Nicole had agreed to give Kim a ride there. They arrived at the house and were kindly greeted by Brother and Sister Cope. After a few moments of conversation, Brother Cope invited Kim to take a seat in a chair in the center of the living room. As Sister Cope and Nicole watched from the couch, Brother Cope placed his hands on Kim's head and began her blessing.

Kim was suddenly a bit apprehensive. How would this man she had just met be able to give her a blessing that would affect her entire life? But a calm feeling settled upon her as she listened to Brother Cope's soothing voice.

Brother Cope told her the Lord was pleased with the choices she had made in her life, especially in recently joining the Church. Then he said, "You come from a noble heritage, and you agreed in the premortal world to be born into the particular family you are in. Your parents are among the very elect of our Heavenly Father's children, and you made a pact to help each other return to your heavenly home."

The words sounded unusual to Kim, as if her dad had once been religious. Then came the words that shook Kim to the core.

"You have a special mission to fulfill. Without you to guide them, your parents will never return to the right path. Stay close to them, in good times as well as bad times. You are the key to their salvation."

Brother Cope continued the blessing. There were comments about being married in the temple and raising a righteous family, but those seemed insignificant at the moment compared to the words about her parents.

When the blessing ended, Kim immediately turned around to face Brother Cope.

"How did you know about my parents?" she asked. "I didn't

even meet you until ten minutes ago. Has the bishop been telling you things?"

Brother Cope smiled. "Not at all. A patriarchal blessing is a message to you from the Lord. I'm just the messenger, so to speak, through the power of the Holy Ghost."

"Well, I just found your words about my parents to be a bit unusual," Kim said. "Partly because they are packed up to move to Nebraska in the morning."

"Aren't you going with them?" Brother Cope asked.

"No, I'm staying with Nicole's family until we graduate, then we're going to be roommates."

"Hmmm," Brother Cope said. "You might want to think that over."

"I certainly will," Kim said.

She and Nicole thanked Brother and Sister Cope, who said they would mail a typed copy of the blessing to Nicole's home in a week or so. The girls then returned to Nicole's car, but Nicole didn't start the engine.

"That was an amazing blessing," Nicole said.

Kim nodded, but frowned a little. "I felt really good about it, except the part about my parents."

"What do you mean?" Nicole asked.

"Didn't it sound like I'm supposed to go with them, rather than stay here?"

"I admit it did," Nicole said. "But you prayed about it, didn't you? You felt you should stay here."

Kim lowered her head. "Um, I guess I never actually got around to praying about it. I just knew it was the right decision."

"Kim! How could you make such a big decision and not pray about it?"

"This praying thing is still new to me," Kim said defensively. "Besides, I was sure that staying here was what Heavenly Father wanted me to do—until now."

They were both silent for several seconds. Finally Nicole softly said, "Maybe this would be a good time to pray about it."

Kim knew she was right. They both bowed their heads, and Kim said, "Heavenly Father, thank you—I mean, thank thee—for all of my blessings. I should've asked sooner, but I feel that the right choice for me is to stay in Utah while my parents go to Nebraska. It will be best for all of us. Um, I ask for your blessing on that."

Kim sat silently, waiting for a warm feeling to pass through her. Instead, she felt dark inside, as if she could hardly breathe. Nicole nudged her and said, "Keep going."

Kim took a deep breath. "Let me rephrase that. Based on the wonderful blessing I just received, I feel the right thing for me is to go to Nebraska with my parents and stay together as a family."

The burden in Kim's chest was suddenly lifted, and she felt able to breathe normally again. She knew that was the right decision.

"Thank you, Heavenly Father," she said, then she reached over and hugged Nicole.

"I'm sad you'll be leaving, but that's where you belong," Nicole said.

The girls embraced for a few more seconds, then Nicole added, "Well, we better see if your parents have any more room in that moving van!"

# Chapter Twenty-Seven

Nicole parked in front of the Marlar home, and Kim ran into the house. She found her parents upstairs packing a few final things.

Kim grabbed Carmen and spun her around. "I'm going with you," she said.

Frank came out of their bedroom. "Thanks, Kim. I appreciate that. I wasn't going to ask you to come all that way to help us unpack, but that would be great."

"No, I don't mean that." She forced a smile. "I'm going to live with you."

Frank and Carmen looked at each other, as if they hadn't heard right. "Say that again?" Carmen asked.

"I've changed my mind. I want to come live in Nebraska."

Frank broke into a grin. "Great!"

He reached out and grabbed Kim in a big hug. Carmen joined them, and Kim felt a rush of joy.

Nicole had come into the house and heard the happy conversation upstairs. She smiled and quietly picked up the phone in the kitchen. Within a few seconds she said, "Hello Elders, this is Nicole Nielsen. If you get this message, Kim Marlar has decided to move to Nebraska with her parents. I thought you might want to say good-bye to her. I imagine we'll be over at my house tonight putting her stuff in the moving van. Hope to see you there."

Within an hour the Marlars' home was empty, and Frank drove

the moving van to Nicole's house. He was backing the van into the driveway when he saw two slightly agitated missionaries hurrying up the sidewalk. Frank put on the parking brake and climbed out as the missionaries crossed the lawn.

"Hello, Elder Brown," Frank said. "Have you heard Kim is going to Nebraska with us?"

"We did," Elder Brown said. "It caught us by surprise."

"Well, at least come tell her good-bye," Frank said. "She's inside the house."

"Thanks, Mr. Marlar. We'll do that."

Kim was excited to see the missionaries, and she invited them to help move her things into the van. The missionaries realized it was Sunday, but they took off their suit coats and pitched in.

"I guess this qualifies as 'an ox in the mire,' right?" Elder Williams asked.

"Sounds like it to me," Elder Brown said.

The work progressed quickly, although each time Kim came into view, Elder Williams had to tell Elder Brown, "Keep your eyes on the work, Elder, not on a certain worker."

Elder Brown would roll his eyes, then would get back to work. Sooner than expected, everything was in the van.

"What are your plans?" Elder Brown asked Frank.

"Well, since we made such good time getting packed, I think we'll head out tonight. We were only staying until Monday so we could be with Kim as long as possible, but now she's going with us, so there's no reason to wait. We'll be taking I-80, and with this big truck, I think I'd rather face the lighter traffic tonight than the morning rush hour. We should be able to make it up the canyon and into Wyoming before stopping at a hotel."

Elder Brown nodded. "That makes sense. Well, I've appreciated your kindness . . ."

Frank couldn't help laughing. "Oh, Elder Brown, to hear you call me 'kind' shows you have a heart of gold."

"No, really! I—"

Frank cut him off by grabbing his hand and giving it a firm

shake. "You're a good man. Stop by if you're ever in Nebraska." Then Frank hobbled off to give Nicole a hug good-bye.

As the rest of the good-byes were said, Elder Brown and Kim just kind of circled away from each other, dreading the actual departure. But soon Frank was starting up the van and Carmen was waiting in their car. At the last moment, Kim gave a hug good-bye to Nicole and promised to call her. Finally, Kim turned to Elder Brown.

"Thanks for everything," she said. "You've changed my life. Let's keep in touch."

She gave him a firm handshake, then hurried to the car, not wanting him to see the tears in her eyes.

# Chapter Twenty-Eight

Many times during the next two months Kim wondered why she had come to Nebraska. Their apartment was small and stuffy, and the kids at her new high school essentially ignored her. She had yet to make a friend there. She called Nicole nearly every night, but her parents didn't mind. They knew they would've been calling Nicole's house often themselves if Kim hadn't come with them.

High school graduation came in late May and Kim went through the motions, not feeling any attachment to her classmates. She had attended the small LDS branch, but she was the only young woman. The branch mainly consisted of young Air Force families with small children, and Kim found herself helping in the nursery each week. She enjoyed it somewhat, but it certainly wasn't spiritually fulfilling. Thankfully, Nicole had mailed her the copy of her patriarchal blessing, and it provided some solace.

Kim's life improved when they finally moved into a home in Omaha. It was now a half-hour drive to the base for Frank, but Kim and Carmen were very pleased. It was a nice neighborhood that reminded them a lot of Layton, minus the mountains. Kim quickly located the ward there in Omaha, and suddenly she felt right at home. The Winter Quarters Temple was north of town, and she would drive there every Sunday evening to walk around the grounds.

One evening in late June there was a knock on the door. Kim peered out the window and saw a nice Nissan parked out front.

"Are either of you expecting visitors?" she asked her parents. They said no, so Kim cautiously opened the door.

"Hi Kim, I was just passing through," said a familiar voice. "Your dad told me to stop by if I was ever in Nebraska."

Kim threw open the door in surprise. "Elder Brown! What are you doing here?"

"I ended my mission a couple of weeks ago and I decided to do some traveling before I got too busy with school and work. By the way, you can call me Josh now."

"Come in . . . Josh! My parents will be glad to see you!"

Kim led Josh into the front room, and Frank and Carmen hopped up as if they were greeting the president of the United States. No one would have ever guessed that this young man had nearly shattered their family just a few months earlier.

Carmen gave Josh a big hug, and Frank just chatted away, reminiscing about that first visit when he'd preferred watching daytime TV to talking with the missionaries.

"I guess you're done with your mission," Carmen said as she eyed his blue jeans and button-down shirt. "No more suits for you!"

Josh smiled. "Not everyday, at least. I'm even letting my hair grow a little."

"I noticed that," Kim said. "I think it looks good."

Frank smiled, noticing the chemistry between Josh and Kim. "Certainly you didn't drive all this way just to see us. What else have you been up to?"

"Like I told Kim, I thought I'd do a little traveling now that my mission is over. You know, before I get into college and all that. My uncle is actually a mission president in New Jersey, and I haven't seen his family in a long time, so I thought I'd just get on I-80 and get there eventually."

"Sounds like fun," Carmen said.

Kim had an idea. "Since you're sightseeing, would you like to see the Winter Quarters Temple? It's not too far from here."

"That would be great," Josh said. "I can drive, if that's all right. Are we all going?"

Kim shot her mother a glance, and Carmen said, "Actually, we've already seen it, right Frank?"

"Uh, right. Say, where are you staying tonight?"

"Oh, I'll find a hotel near the freeway."

"Nonsense," Frank said. "When you get back here we'll have a bed ready for you on the couch. Then we can play a game or something."

"Thanks so much, Mr. Marlar," Josh said with a smile. "I always appreciated your kindness . . ."

"Aw, get out of here!" Frank said, slapping Josh on the back. "You two have fun."

❦

The ride to the temple was filled with excited conversation as they filled each other in on the past few weeks. Kim told Josh about her horrible final weeks of high school, and he sympathized just as she hoped he would.

When they arrived at the temple, they walked slowly around it. "I can't wait until I can go inside," Kim said. "I'm eager to get Tina's temple work done, but they are making me wait a year after her death to do it."

"When will that be?" Josh asked.

"September 6th. I plan on doing the baptism myself, but then I don't know who could do the rest of the ordinances."

"My sister Becky will be home from her mission in the Canary Islands by then," Josh said. "I've written to her about you and your family. She'd be honored to do the work."

"Really? I'll keep that in mind."

They sat together on the lawn on the east side of the temple. The floodlights had just come on, and the temple seemed to shimmer as the sun set behind it.

"It's so beautiful," Kim said. "I don't think I can thank you enough for teaching me the gospel. Without you, I'd really be lost, especially now that we've moved to Nebraska. Who knows if I would've ever found the church."

Josh felt his pulse racing, trying to keep his emotions in check.

"Kim, I've never really told you about the day I left that Book of Mormon on your porch. We had actually walked past your house with no intention of knocking on your door. Then suddenly it felt like I ran into an invisible wall. I couldn't move forward. Elder Rhees thought I was nuts, but I just knew we had to knock on that door." He smiled and added, "Of course, after meeting your father, I questioned my spiritual sensitivity."

Kim tried to smack him on the arm. "You be nice!"

Josh blocked her swing and found himself holding her hand. She didn't pull away. Instead she asked, "Then what made you leave a Book of Mormon on the porch of an ornery man?"

Josh shrugged. "Once again, it came from outside of me, like a voice. Maybe someone is watching over you from the other side."

Kim was touched. "Maybe so."

They soon walked around the rest of the temple, but neither one let go of the other's hand—or acknowledged it, either.

Finally they returned to the car and Kim said, "Elder Brown, I mean Josh, thanks for taking the time to visit us. I hope you enjoy your trip to the East Coast."

"I will," Josh said, but he was already liking the Midwest just fine.

❧

They returned to find that Kim's parents had already set up a game of Trivial Pursuit at the table, and had drinks and candy waiting. For the next hour they had a fun time, although Kim had a sneaking suspicion Josh missed a couple of questions at the end so Frank could surge ahead for a surprise victory.

The next morning Josh was up early and ready to hit the road. He gave Frank a handshake, gave Carmen a hug, then gave Kim a handshake, too. "Maybe I'll stop by in a few weeks on my way back," he said, and they all told him they'd love to see him again.

At the breakfast table after he left, Kim was unusually quiet. "What's wrong, dear?" Carmen asked.

"I just miss him already, that's all," Kim said, looking into her cereal bowl.

Frank winked at Carmen, then said, "Josh is a perfectly fine boy with a nice car, but he doesn't have a job or any education."

Kim's eyes shot up. "You watch! He'll make something of himself!"

Frank smiled. "I'm sure he will."

# CHAPTER TWENTY-NINE

Five nights later there was another knock on the Marlars' door. Kim opened the door and was relieved to see Josh standing there. She invited him in, and called to her parents, who were in the kitchen.

"Maybe now Kim will stop moping around," Carmen whispered to her husband.

They gathered in the living room, and Josh explained he'd made it to New Jersey, but after one day he'd seen enough. "My uncle wanted me to go work all day with the missionaries! I told him, 'What do you think I just did for two years?'"

Frank gave a laugh. "That's right. You deserve a rest!"

"That's how I felt," Josh said with a smile. "Besides, I had such a fun time with you guys, I thought I'd head back this way."

"Well, you know you're welcome to stay here again," Carmen said.

"That would be nice."

Kim quietly watched their conversation, and for the first time in days her heart felt light. After a while, Frank and Carmen excused themselves.

"Now don't stay up too late," Frank said as he closed their bedroom door.

Kim and Josh suddenly found themselves alone, and words were hard to come by. Finally Josh asked, "So what are your plans for the next little while?"

Kim sighed. "Mom wants me to find a job, but there really isn't much here. I'd probably end up working in a fast-food joint. Dad makes good money, so it's not crucial for me to work. Lately I've just been doing a lot of reading. There's a good library just down the road. They even have some LDS stuff."

"That's very good," Josh said, a bit distracted. "Say . . . I was just wondering . . ."

Kim looked up expectantly. "Yes?"

Josh laughed. "What I'm trying to say is . . ."

"I really like you, Josh," Kim said suddenly.

"Yeah, that's it—without the Josh part," he said with a chuckle. "I think we really get along well, don't you?"

Kim nodded. "It feels like I've known you forever, and I guess we have known each other for several months."

Josh shifted and faced her. "Well, here's the real story. I did spend a few hours working with the missionaries in New Jersey, but the whole time I was there, I was wishing I was back in Omaha, Nebraska. I also felt that way driving there and back, and believe me, it wasn't because I wanted to be with your father."

Kim laughed. "Why, thank you. For what it's worth, my mother will gladly tell you I haven't been very pleasant to be around since you left."

"So where does that leave us?" Josh asked.

Kim shrugged. "Well, we've shook hands a lot, and I guess at the temple we held hands. But now I'm wishing for a hug."

Josh smiled and quickly fulfilled her wish, along with a kiss.

❧

Kim and Josh spent essentially every moment of the next week together, and they realized they couldn't bear to be apart. Josh had unofficially proposed to Kim, and she had unofficially said yes. They hadn't told her parents, though, partially because of the logistics. They had taken several long walks to discuss their future. Josh wanted Kim to move to California, but she wouldn't budge.

They returned to the house after spending the morning at a park. Carmen had left a note that she was at the store, and Frank was at work. Josh decided to press the issue about California once more. After a few tense words, Josh finally asked, "What have you got against California?"

"Nothing." Kim then asked him to wait a moment as she found her scripture case. Then she pulled out her patriarchal blessing and allowed him to read it. As he got to the part about her parents, he finally understood.

"Nicole had mentioned you needed to be with your parents," Josh said. "I can see why."

Kim was on the verge of tears. "I love you, but I feel I would be breaking some sort of eternal covenant if I just took off to California. Yet I don't feel you should have to leave your family, either. You've been gone for two years already."

Josh felt his insides knot up. "Maybe we should take a break. I'll drive home, and then we'll see how we are feeling."

Kim smiled through teary eyes. "I already know I'll be miserable after you leave, but I think that's the best decision."

Josh gave her a long kiss, grabbed his suitcase, then went to his car. Kim went to the couch and collapsed in tears.

❧

Kim didn't hear from Josh for a full week. In the meantime, she told her parents how serious she and Josh had become. They had already suspected as much, and they really couldn't see a reason to object. They had married young, too, and they knew it wasn't a big issue. Plus, they knew Josh would treat Kim right.

Frank's biggest concern was that they might be rushing things. He told Kim to wait for several months before setting a wedding date. Carmen disagreed, partly because Kim was rarely happy without Josh around.

As the argument escalated, Carmen asked, "Frank, how long did we wait to get married after we met?"

"I'm not going to answer that," he said with a hint of defiance. "Things were different then."

"How long was it?" Kim asked, enjoying seeing her father on the defensive.

"A month."

"What?" Carmen exclaimed. "Tell the truth."

"Well, we met on May 20th and got married on June 3rd," he said. "I know I turned a page of the calendar somewhere in there."

Kim laughed. "See? I've known Josh for several months, and we don't even have to exaggerate about it."

Frank sensed he was losing the battle, but he still had some points to make. "You don't have a job, and Josh isn't in school or working, either. You aren't going to live here, that's for sure."

"Of course not."

"Well, until both of those things are cleared up—jobs or school—I can't give my approval," Frank said. "But if they are . . ."

Kim leaped up and into her father's arms. "Oh, thank you. I'll get a job. I promise!"

෨

The long-awaited phone call from Josh finally came, and it was worth the wait.

"Kim, I've been checking into colleges all around Omaha, and I think my best bet is Kansas State University in Manhattan, Kansas. My dad has friends there, and he made some calls. He thinks they could get me in for fall classes if I get my application sent in by the end of the week. The school is a half-day's drive from your parents' house, but that's still a lot closer to them than California."

Kim felt a tingle go through her. "That sounds great! I've talked a lot to my parents this week, and believe it or not, they're very supportive of us being together. Dad just wants to make sure you're in school and that I have a job."

"That sounds reasonable," Josh said.

"How about your parents?" Kim asked. "What did you tell them?"

Josh gave a tired laugh. "Well, they think I'm crazy and that it's just a mission crush. But once I made it clear I'm in love and determined to go forward, they didn't have much to say. They would like to meet you before the wedding, though."

Kim laughed. "We can work that out."

"My father just wanted to make sure I got my education," Josh said. "I think Kansas State will work out best."

# CHAPTER THIRTY

During the first week of July, Kim and Carmen flew out to San Diego, and they spent a few days with Josh's family. Josh's parents, Daniel and Heather, were quite impressed with Kim. Within two days they were acting as if she had always been a part of the family. Josh took Kim down near the ocean, where he officially knelt before her and gave her a beautiful diamond ring.

In the previous weeks, Josh had resolved a concern that had been nagging at him. Kim had only been a member of the Church for a few months, but they wanted a temple marriage. So with his stake president's help, they followed the proper priesthood channels and approval was given for Josh and Kim to be sealed in the temple before the year mark of her baptism.

Their stake presidents agreed this marriage did present a rare exception, since Kim was fully worthy and had only delayed taking the missionary discussions because of her parents' wishes. The church leaders couldn't see any reason why this young couple should have to postpone their temple marriage on such a technicality.

Once the engagement was official, the couple's mothers decided the time had come to really begin planning the wedding. That night they met around the Brown family's dining room table.

"What day do you begin school?" Heather asked her son.

"September 15th," Josh said. "But of course we'd want a honeymoon."

"Your sister Becky won't return from her mission until September 1st. We certainly would want her here, so it can't be sooner than that."

136

Kim asked, "How about September 6th?"

Heather checked the calendar. "That's a Saturday. I don't see why not. Is there a special reason?"

Carmen tenderly said, "That's the day my younger daughter Tina died."

"Yes," Kim said. "It would make the day so much more wonderful if Tina's temple work could be done on the day of our wedding."

"That sounds perfect," Heather said.

❧

The next two months were a whirlwind, with lots of calls between San Diego and Omaha. Kim traveled to California three times, and she ended up spending almost as much time there as in Nebraska during the next few weeks.

Then on September 4th Frank and Carmen boarded a plane and arrived in San Diego. That night the Browns invited them over to finalize any last-minute details. As the Marlars arrived, an older man hopped off the couch and grabbed Frank's hand.

"Hello, Mr. Marlar! I'm Tex Brown, Josh's grandpa. It's always nice to meet another member of the Armed Services."

Frank immediately felt a kinship with Tex. "You can call me Frank. If you don't mind me asking, what branch of the service were you in?"

"The Army during World War II," Tex said.

"I would've guessed you're much younger than that," he said.

"You're just being polite," Tex said with a smile. "I spent a few months in a German prison camp, which aged me considerably. It wasn't all bad, though. That's where I found the LDS Church—and my wife. I'll have to tell you about it sometime."

"That's a unique combination," Frank said, looking around. "Is your wife here?"

Tex frowned slightly. "Ingrid passed away last year."

"I'm so sorry to hear that," Frank said. "We lost a daughter a year ago, too, and it's still a struggle."

Just then a beautiful brunette walked in the room, and Tex motioned to her. "Becky, come meet the Marlars."

"Josh has told me so much about you," Carmen said as Becky shook hands with them.

"I hope he only had good things to say," she said with a grin. "I just got back from the Canary Islands, so if I say something in Spanish, please forgive me. My English is just coming back."

Josh stuck his head in and called them to the dinner table. "We've got all night to talk. Let's get eating!"

✺

The following night some of Josh's old buddies gave him an LDS bachelor party. As Becky had explained to the group the night before, "They'll just sit around, eat pizza and swap mission stories. Really wild stuff!"

Carmen and Frank preferred to just go back to their hotel and sit by the pool, so Becky offered to give Kim a tour of San Diego while the boys were off having their "fun." They drove all over, including past the San Diego Temple where the wedding would take place the following day. They eventually ended up at La Jolla Cove, a beautiful beach nestled between craggy cliffs. They parked the car and walked down to the water's edge, watching the waves roll in at sunset. Kim was surprised at how quickly she had formed a bond with Becky, and told her so.

"I feel the same about you," Becky said, "although I always knew it would take someone special to marry Josh. He's one of a kind."

A thought came to Kim. "As you might know, my sister Tina died last year. Tomorrow is actually the anniversary of her death."

"Yes, Josh told me that."

"Well, I have an ordinance card printed with her information on it, and I have been hoping that her temple work could be done tomorrow. Since I'll be receiving my own endowment tomorrow, would you be willing to complete her temple work while we're in the temple?"

"That would be great," Becky said. "I'm touched you would have me be the one to do her work."

As they sat on the beach, Kim told Becky some of the details of how she and Josh had ended up together. Becky shook her head and said, "I wish I had such a clear-cut answer."

"What do you mean?"

"Well, before I went on my mission, I was basically dating two guys at the same time," Becky said.

"That doesn't sound like a problem—or a surprise," Kim said. "You're beautiful. I'm sure you had a lot of guys after you."

Becky shrugged off the compliment. "I went on my mission for the right reasons, but I also went in hopes that one of them would get married while I was gone. Unfortunately, they're both still single, and both eager to see me."

Kim smiled. "Tell me a little bit about them."

"We'll start with Chris. We dated for nearly a year. He's making pretty good money playing basketball in Europe, and he still has hopes of making the NBA."

"That sounds pretty good," Kim said.

"I suppose," Becky said without enthusiasm. "The other guy, Doug, is a student at BYU that I dated a few times just before my mission. He's a returned missionary—which Chris isn't—and we've been sending letters to each other. But Doug wants to become a writer, and I don't know many rich authors."

"Do you have to make a decision right now?" Kim asked.

"Fairly soon. I have to make up my mind whether to fly to France to visit Chris, or re-enroll at BYU for winter semester, where I'm certain to see Doug again."

Kim nodded thoughtfully. "Well, if money was really what mattered, you'd already have your airline tickets, wouldn't you?"

"Yeah," Becky admitted.

Then Kim asked, "Which guy makes you a better person? Which one makes you laugh?"

"Am I supposed to base my future on that?" Becky asked.

"Yes, if you're not basing your decision on money."

Becky squinted into the setting sun. "There really isn't a comparison between the two. Chris isn't much of a gentleman. In fact, he treats me kind of like a slave. I certainly feel better about myself when I'm around Doug. He has a calm maturity, and he treats me so well. Plus, Grandpa Tex hates Chris, but seems to think Doug is the greatest guy in the world."

"It doesn't hurt to have your family like your husband," Kim said.

Becky grabbed a handful of sand and let it run through her fingers. "I guess after being so poor on the Canary Islands for 18 months, I've let the big salary Chris receives play a larger role in my decision than it should. The poverty on the islands was depressing, and I vowed to marry a rich guy. Naturally, my thoughts turned to Chris, but in every other way Doug comes out ahead."

"I can relate to that. I'm marrying your brother, and it's definitely not for the money," Kim said jokingly before adding, "It sounds like you've made your decision."

Becky smiled. "Yes, I believe I have."

# CHAPTER THIRTY-ONE

Tina and Nimhi were standing atop a small hill, teaching a group of nearly 800 ancestors about Joseph Smith. This group had been living deep in the jungles of the Spirit World and had only recently come to Nimhi's city. They had been found by Nimhi's servants, who were now searching the jungle for people to teach.

This group was very receptive to the gospel message, just like the dozens of other groups Tina had taught. She estimated 25,000 spirits had accepted the gospel. They were now all waiting to have baptisms performed for them so they could enter Paradise.

Nimhi told the group how the Lord had restored the Church of Jesus Christ to the earth in the latter days. "By accepting Christ and the teachings Sister Tina has brought us," Nimhi said, "we will someday have the chance to travel beyond the horizon and enter Paradise."

Shouts of approval came from the crowd, and Tina smiled. Nimhi had become a masterful teacher. Suddenly a radiant white-robed spirit appeared, and the crowd gasped as Lucille slowly lowered herself beside Tina.

"The long-awaited day has finally arrived," Lucille told her granddaughter. "A baptism will be performed in your behalf today in the San Diego Temple."

"San Diego?" Tina asked. "California?"

"Yes," Lucille said. "Many exciting things have happened in your family since you last visited the mortal world. We need to leave soon, but certainly take a moment to say good-bye."

Nimhi knew this moment would eventually come. He grasped

Tina's arm and said, "Thank you for all you have done for my people. We will remember you forever."

Lucille was pleasantly surprised at Nimhi's appearance. The flashy robe was gone. Instead he now wore a plain, off-white robe. He also was no longer constantly followed by servants. Instead, he spent his time teaching the gospel to others.

Tina gave Nimhi a small embrace. "Carry on the great work you're doing," she said. "I'll be back soon, hopefully to lead you and all of these people into Paradise."

⚘

On the way back across the Spirit World, Lucille told Tina about Kim and Josh. Tina was happily surprised to hear that not only would she be having her temple work done today, but so would Kim.

"I still can't believe my father allowed this," Tina said.

"Miracles happen," Lucille said as they braced themselves to pop through the veil. They emerged above the San Diego Temple, and Lucille escorted Tina immediately to the baptismal font. Kim was standing at the edge of the font, waiting her turn, with Josh standing beside her. They were both dressed in white.

"Your sister must truly love you to start her wedding day like this," Lucille said. "Kim will be baptized and confirmed in your behalf, then Josh's sister Becky will do the remainder of your temple work today."

As Kim and Josh entered the water, a kindly spirit woman motioned Tina forward to watch from the edge of the font. It wasn't much different than when she had watched Josh baptize Kim. But this time it was for her! Paradise was within her grasp!

Tina watched carefully as the baptism was performed, and she noticed there were two witnesses in the mortal world, and also two in the spirit world to acknowledge her acceptance of the baptism. As Kim came out of the water, one of the nearby spirits asked, "Do you accept this baptism in your behalf?"

"Yes," Tina said. "With all my soul!"

After drying off and changing into a white dress, Kim was confirmed a member of the Church for Tina, who was standing nearby. Kim then gave the temple card to Becky, who acted in Tina's behalf during the rest of the temple ordinances. Tina was right by Becky's side the whole time, and she eagerly accepted the truths she was being taught.

When Becky finally entered the Celestial Room, Tina thanked her profusely. At that moment Becky looked into a large mirror and saw the reflection of a beautiful dark-haired woman mouthing the words "Thank you" to her. Becky looked around, but the woman was nowhere to be seen. She looked again in the mirror, but the woman was no longer visible. Becky's heart gave a leap.

When Kim entered the Celestial Room a few moments later, Becky whispered to her, "I never thought of it, since you have blonde hair and blue eyes, but did Tina have darker skin and hair like your mother?"

"Yes."

Becky's eyes welled up with tears. "I just saw her in a mirror. She seemed very pleased about what we've done for her."

A lump rose into Kim's throat. "Thanks for sharing that. I just know Tina has accepted the gospel."

There was little time to talk, though, as the group soon moved to a sealing room. In the center of the room was a beautiful altar. Josh and Kim knelt across from each other and became husband and wife for time and all eternity.

Tina was allowed to attend the sealing, and she was pleased to see Grandpa and Grandma Marlar there, as well as Ingrid Brown, Josh's deceased grandma. As the sealing concluded, the man who performed the ordinance raised his hands for silence. He then said, "I have felt the presence of several spirits who have come from across the veil to be with us today. If you have loved ones who would have been here if they hadn't passed to the other side, be assured they were here with you today to share in your happiness."

᠕

Carmen and Frank had spent the morning waiting in the temple's visitors center. They had watched several videos and Carmen was feeling very good inside, despite the disappointment of not being able to attend her daughter's wedding. She turned to Frank and asked, "Do you think we'll ever be able to go inside the temple?"

Frank made a face. "These Mormons are nice people, but don't get your hopes up."

Carmen said nothing more, sensing her husband's anti-Mormon feelings were flaring up again. Little did she know his reaction came more out of guilt than anything else.

# Chapter Thirty-Two

"Well, are you ready to see your new home?" Lucille asked Tina as the mortals left the sealing room.

"You mean . . ."

"Yes, Paradise awaits you."

Tina paused. "Can I say good-bye to Ida first?"

"Certainly."

The rushed back to Spirit Prison, where Ida met them in the lobby of the apartment complex. "Congratulations," Ida said through a tearful smile. "I've heard you are moving on."

Tina hugged her and whispered, "Kim is going to find your records. I just know it!"

There was suddenly a rustle next to them as Ruby appeared. She gave Tina a shove.

"Why didn't you listen to me? Paradise is all a lie," Ruby sneered. "You'll get over there and see it is worse than here. You're making a mistake!"

Tina turned her back on Ruby without a word. "Grandma, I'm ready."

Lucille nodded and they zoomed out the door. Ida returned to her room, leaving Ruby shouting vile words at no one in particular.

Within moments they reached the edge of the Great Gulf, and two large angels approached them. They asked Tina certain questions, and after having been in the temple, Tina could answer them easily. The angels smiled, and they motioned her to go forward. Tina reached out for Lucille's hand.

"Here we go," Tina said. "Lead the way."

They floated quickly over the Great Gulf, and on the horizon a magnificent land appeared. The vegetation was more alive and colorful than in Spirit Prison, and the buildings were more splendid. Wonderful music praising Heavenly Father drifted through the air. Lucille guided her past a sprawling community and to the top of a large hill. On the hill stood the most beautiful home Tina had ever seen.

"Who lives here?" she asked.

"We do."

Lucille guided her to the front door, and as they entered she motioned to a large bedroom. "This is your room until your mansion is built," she told Tina.

She then allowed Tina to explore the whole house, and it was fantastic. Tina's favorite part was a greenhouse in the center of the home that was filled with all kinds of exotic plants. But she was surprised when a large dog leaped out from under a bush.

"Grandma, there's a dog in here," Tina called out.

She turned back to the dog, who shocked her by saying, "I won't hurt you. My name is Zipper."

Grandma arrived, and Tina asked, "What is going on? I haven't seen any animals in the Spirit World, and now I'm suddenly talking to a dog?"

Both Grandma and Zipper laughed. Grandma walked over to Zipper and scratched his head. "Zipper was our family's favorite pet on earth, and he has been allowed to live with us. Animals have spirits too, and they have their own section of the Spirit World. But spirits in Paradise can request to have their pets come live with them. If the animal agrees, everything works out just fine."

Tina shrugged. "Makes sense to me."

"I'm glad to finally meet you," Zipper said. "Everyone is so happy you are here." Then he trotted back under the bush.

Tina smiled. "Zipper seems to be quite a character."

"He's a lot of fun," Lucille said. "Zipper and your dad really loved each other, and he hopes your dad makes it here."

"I think we are all hoping for that."

Lucille took her by the hand. "Before you get settled, I've got one more place to show you."

They left the house and flew farther into Paradise. The overall beauty of the landscape and buildings were nearly overwhelming, but they didn't prepare Tina for the sight that loomed ahead.

A mountain seemingly made of diamonds towered above them, and a majestic golden city lay below it, ringed by a fiery fence.

"This is where the Savior lives when he visits Paradise," Lucille said.

"It's unbelievable," Tina said. "I've never seen such beauty!"

They could see white-robed people walking around in the city. "Can we go in?" Tina asked.

"Maybe someday, when we are called to do so," Lucille said. "Prophets such as Joseph Smith and Brigham Young live there, as well as the early prophets, such as Adam and Noah. They are all working together to prepare the world for the Second Coming. It isn't far off, you know."

They gazed at the city for a long time, both hoping to go there soon. Finally Lucille said, "It's time to go back. The council wanted to meet with you again."

# CHAPTER THIRTY-THREE

They crossed the Great Gulf and waited patiently for their turn to meet with the council. When they were beckoned in, Brother Dalton said, "Congratulations, Tina. We're all pleased you have entered Paradise. Sadly, you won't be here long."

"What do you mean?" Tina asked.

"We want you to return to the mortal world," Brother Dalton said. "Your sister Kim is the first baptized member of your family to live in Kansas, and this is the first real chance Ida has had to be discovered in more than a century. But Kim obviously has no knowledge of her. The council wants you to somehow motivate her to research her family history."

"I look forward to it."

"Do you think you can still resist tinkering with the mortal world?" Brother Dalton asked.

Tina grinned. "I'll do my best."

Tina soon found herself back on earth, and this was her most difficult adjustment yet. She missed the overwhelming feelings of love she'd felt in Paradise, but she would do anything to help Ida.

Tina knew Ida's earthly records only existed in one place—on a faded, handwritten card in the courthouse in Osborne, Kansas. The card was in a wooden box that hadn't been opened in more than forty years. Somehow Tina had to guide Kim to those records.

The task turned out to be more difficult than Tina had ever expected. Kim and Josh had rented a small apartment a few miles from the Kansas State campus. Kim had taken a job as a telemarketer during the day while Josh was at school. So for eight hours a day—plus a half-hour each way on the bus—Kim was essentially unresponsive to Tina's promptings. Then once she was home, Kim would hurriedly make dinner in time for Josh to arrive. Then they'd spend the night talking about their day, working on Josh's school assignments, or going to a movie. It was obvious they were in love and deserved to be focused on each other, but Tina felt she might never make a breakthrough.

One Sunday morning as Tina followed Kim into Relief Society, she prayed something in the lesson would trigger Kim's interest. Tina had attended church with Kim the previous three weeks, and no one had come even close to talking about family history— unless you count the older sisters telling the younger sisters how much better things were "in the good old days."

On this day an ancient lady named Sister Olsen stood before the class to teach the lesson. It looked like she might topple over any minute, and Tina's hopes were wavering. Then Sister Olsen wrote on the chalkboard, "Redeeming the Dead."

"I realize most of you have already done the temple work for all of your ancestors," Sister Olsen said. "So this lesson might not mean much to you, but it is an important part of the gospel. Is there anyone here who hasn't completed their four-generation pedigree chart?"

Kim looked around. No other hands went up, but she meekly put her hand in the air.

"You there in the corner," Sister Olsen said, looking at Kim. "How come you haven't done your four-generation chart?"

Kim shrugged. "I don't know what one is."

A flurry of whispers filled the room, and Sister Olsen looked like she was in shock. "Surely your mother filled one out," she said. Kim shook her head, and the woman hastily pulled a piece of paper out of her binder.

"Pass this back to that girl," she told a woman on the front row. The paper finally reached Kim. It had a tree-like structure printed on it.

"It's like your family tree," the woman next to Kim whispered.

Sister Olsen told Kim, "Just fill that out and bring it next week." "You better do as she says," the woman whispered. "She's a fanatic about it, and she'll pester you until you show her you've done it."

Then Sister Olsen moved on to another topic, never returning again to "Redeeming the Dead." A heated discussion began about how men don't do anything around the house during football season, but Tina was smiling as Kim ignored the discussion and carefully studied the chart.

❧

After Relief Society, Kim met Josh in the hall. "Why don't we go see my parents today?" she asked.

Josh frowned a little. "That's a four-hour drive. Couldn't we just call them?"

"Maybe, but I want to talk to them about this." Kim showed him the four-generation sheet. "We talked about it in class, and I can't fill out any of it except my name and my parents' names. That doesn't feel right."

Josh nodded. "Well, let them know we're coming, then we can go."

"Thanks so much," Kim said, giving him a kiss. They called her parents, who were excited to hear they would be visiting.

During the drive, Josh answered all of her questions about family history work. He even had her read section 138 in the Doctrine and Covenants, which discusses how the Spirit World operates.

Kim said, "How come you never told me this?"

Josh shrugged. "I guess we've been so busy falling in love and getting married, it never crossed my mind."

They reached Omaha in mid-afternoon, and as they entered the house they discovered Carmen had prepared a splendid meal. All thoughts of family history were forgotten as they downed steaks with potatoes and gravy.

"This is wonderful," Josh said. "We need to come here more often!"

Carmen looked at the paper Kim had been carrying around since their arrival. "What's that, dear?" she asked.

"Oh, it's just something they handed out at Church," Kim said. "I'm hoping you can help me with it. I have to get it filled out or an old woman will be breathing down my neck about it."

The others didn't notice Frank stiffen as Kim smoothed the paper out. "It's called a four-generation pedigree chart where you keep track of your family," she said. "I only have two generations— me and you two. Do you remember much about your parents or grandparents?"

Carmen studied the paper. "Well, my parents are Hernando and Ana Ramos. I know their birthdays, but I don't know what year they were born." She stared at the ceiling in concentration. "When I was young, my papa's mother lived with us, but we just called her 'Grandma.' I don't remember much else."

"Well, that's a start," Kim said as she wrote Carmen's parents' names onto the paper. Then she turned to her father. "How about you, Dad?"

"I don't remember my parents," Frank said flatly.

"Is that why you've never mentioned them?" Kim asked, concerned.

Frank shrugged and let out a long sigh. "I didn't want to dig up the past—all those foster homes . . ."

Tina had also made the trip to Omaha, and she was furious at Frank. "He's lying," she shouted into Kim's ear. "Grandpa and Grandma Marlar are wonderful people. They love him!"

Kim was momentarily distracted, but then she said, "Certainly you have a record of their names."

Frank shook his head. "I don't think so."

Suddenly Carmen brightened. "Hey, it's probably on your birth certificate!"

Frank's eyes darted briefly, but then he said, "Hey, you're probably right." Then he slapped his palm to his head. "Carmen, don't you remember? We searched for it several years ago when we were in Japan."

Carmen looked at Kim. "We couldn't ever find it."

Frank looked sadly into Kim's eyes. "I've always wanted to find my real family, but I don't think it's possible."

Kim felt uneasy. Something wasn't right, but she knew better than to push him. Meanwhile, Tina was so angry at Frank that she zoomed out of the house rather than throw the gravy container on him.

Josh and Kim returned to Kansas late that night. It had been nice to see her parents, but Kim was disappointed that all she had gotten were two names and no actual dates. It felt like her parents had just sprung up out of nowhere—as if they were people without a past.

As they settled into bed, Josh said, "Well, at least your father turned out all right. I've known a few people who didn't do so well in foster care. We should be grateful for that."

Kim just nodded as the uneasy feeling returned.

❧

The next day after Josh went to school, Kim called in sick to work and went straight to the public library, feeling there had to be a record of her father's parents somewhere. She talked with a librarian about finding family records, and the librarian said the Internet was the best place to find information like that.

Kim found an empty Internet terminal and although she didn't have much computer experience, she was able to do a search for "Marlar." She realized it might not be her father's real last name, but at least it was a place to start. To her surprise, a website was listed that was entirely devoted to several generations of the Marlar family. It was a very simple website, but it was quite functional. Kim scrolled down and saw the listings for two men with the name Frank. Benjamin Franklin Marlar and Frank Marlar.

She clicked on the first name and information came on the

screen about a man who lived in the 1800s. There was a full-page biography and a lengthy list of descendants.

"I don't think that's him," Kim said to herself. She clicked on the other name, and three lines came onto the screen:

Frank Marlar
Born: 22 May 1959
Parents: Samuel and Lucille Marlar

"Yes!" Kim shouted, startling a few patrons. That was her father's birthdate. It couldn't be a coincidence. She jotted down Frank's parents' names, returned to the main listing of names, then sat in stunned silence. The listing showed that both of Frank's parents had been born and died in Utah.

Kim finally said, "That is really bizarre. Maybe they were even members of the Church."

Kim spent the next hour searching the website, and her excitement grew. Several generations of the Marlar family had lived in Osborne, Kansas, a small town about 150 miles west of her apartment. She printed off as much information as she could. A new passion had come alive in her that she couldn't quite explain.

When Josh arrived home that evening, Kim had the Marlar information spread out on the table.

"Hi, dear," she said. "I took the day off work and went to the library. Look at what I found."

Josh shook off his surprise that she had skipped work and peered at the papers on the table. "What is it exactly?"

"It's my father's family!" She handed him the sheet that detailed her father's parents, and Josh had to sit down.

"From Utah?" he asked. "Wow, that's a shock."

"Yes, I'm sure Dad will be surprised."

"Have you called him?"

"I tried," Kim said, "but there wasn't an answer. They probably went out to eat. But I'm so excited! I'm going to need the car in the morning to do a little more research. Can I drop you off at school?"

"You aren't going to work tomorrow either?"

"I can't," Kim said, jumping up and down. "I wouldn't be able to focus. It's like I've discovered my long-lost family. Can I just take the car?"

"Where are you going?" Josh asked.

"There's a little town not far from here that might hold all of my family secrets. I just want to drive over there and see what kind of records they have."

Josh knew he wouldn't win this battle. "Oh, all right."

Kim decided against calling her father again, figuring she'd share all her discoveries after she returned from her trip. She was certain he'd be pleased she had discovered his family line.

❧

The next morning Kim dropped off Josh and headed west. She hadn't felt the need to tell him how far it actually was to Osborne. It was now 8 a.m., and Josh expected her to pick him up at 4 p.m. She figured it would take about three hours to get to Osborne, and then three hours back, leaving her two hours to do research. She planned on submitting the temple work of anyone she could verify as being related to her.

"What has gotten into me?" she said with a laugh.

Tina smiled at her sister's enthusiasm from the passenger seat. "Just keep it up," Tina told her.

Kim pulled to a stop in front of the tiny Osborne courthouse just after 11 a.m. It was empty except for a middle-aged man in the city clerk's office. The man put down his pen and said, "How can I help you?"

Kim read the nameplate on his desk. "Hello . . . Dave. I'm here to find some records about the Marlar family."

"That name sounds familiar," Dave said as he hopped up and went to a filing cabinet. He handed Kim a listing of people buried in the cemetery. Kim was pleased to see many Marlar names on the list. Dave let her photocopy it so she could compare it with the records she had found on the Internet. Kim then spent several minutes at the front counter matching the names in the two records.

By now it was noon, and Dave said he was closing for a half-hour so he could go home for lunch.

"Can't I just stay?" Kim asked. "I won't cause trouble."

Dave hesitated before saying, "While I'm gone, why don't you drive down the street to the cemetery and see if you can account for everyone. It's not far."

"That's a good idea," Kim said, and she waved good-bye as Dave locked the door and walked down the sidewalk. Kim easily found the cemetery, and near the center was a thick, eight-foot high granite marker that read, "Marlar."

The Marlar plot seemed to form a square. The people buried there all seemed to match up with the information she had found on the Internet. Kim shuffled though her papers and began checking off each person. Some of the stones were hard to read, but she was able to account for everyone on her list.

However, there was an extra, crumbling tombstone in the very center of the lot that didn't have a name on it. She double-checked the photocopy Dave had given her, but there wasn't an extra name on the list. It seemed peculiar that a tombstone would be unaccounted for, but maybe Dave had another record in the courthouse that would tell her who was buried there.

Tina tried to get Kim's attention. "Look more closely," she begged. To Tina, it was obvious that the stone read Ida Marlar, but to Kim's mortal eyes it wasn't readable.

Kim checked her watch and gasped. "12:30 already!" She felt like she had just gotten there, but she would have to leave within half an hour. She hurried back to the courthouse and explained to Dave she had discovered an extra tombstone.

"That's strange," Dave said. "I thought we'd figured out who everyone was in the cemetery long ago. Not too many people get buried there now, so it's pretty easy to keep track."

"Well, I'd like to know who that person was," Kim said. "Maybe it belongs to one of my father's grandparents."

Dave grew thoughtful, then said, "Follow me."

He led her to a cluttered back room and kicked some junk away from a closet door. "I probably shouldn't do this, but what can it hurt?" he asked.

He pulled open the closet, and the hinges screeched from lack of use. Dave pointed to a large wooden box on the closet's top shelf. "That box holds all of the original death information for everyone ever buried in the cemetery."

Dave pulled the box down, placed it on a table, and wiped the dust off the lid with a rag. As he lifted the lid, Kim could see a row of index cards running along the bottom of the box.

"I really ought to get this stuff typed into a database, but I haven't gotten to it yet," Dave said.

The phone rang.

"I better get that," Dave said. "Go ahead and start looking. They should be in alphabetical order. Just be careful not to mix them up."

Kim reached into the box, and Tina stood excitedly nearby. She could hardly believe how easily it had all come together! Ida's long stay in Spirit Prison was finally going to end.

Within a few moments Kim found the Marlar cards, and she pulled them out as if they were gold. She carefully placed the stack of two dozen cards on the table and began to check each one.

"There's George Marlar," Kim said aloud as she made a checkmark on her printout. "Then Harry Marlar . . . then Jane Marlar . . ."

Tina felt a small shiver. Why wasn't Ida's name mentioned? Tina carefully looked at Harry Marlar's card and panic filled her. That card was actually two cards stuck together! The second one had to be Ida's card!

Without a second thought, Tina reached out to pull the cards apart, but in her haste she accidentally pushed the whole stack off the table. Tina stood helplessly as Kim let out a soundless cry.

Dave was still talking on the phone in the other room, so Kim scrambled to the floor, gathered up the cards, and hurriedly got them back into order. "Oh no," she said to herself. "Where's Harry Marlar's card?"

She searched frantically, but it was nowhere to be found. Just then Dave hung up the phone, so Kim put the Marlar cards back in the box and closed the lid.

"I'm all done," she said pleasantly. "Everything checks out. Maybe someday I'll figure out who that extra tombstone belongs to."

Dave smiled. "I'm glad I could help."

"Well, I better head home," Kim told him, knowing she would barely make it back to the university in time to pick up Josh.

Dave put the box back on the closet shelf and they left the room, unaware that Tina was sprawled on the floor in tears. She was reaching down through a floor vent, trying in vain to grab two cards that had slipped through the grate. The cards listed the death dates of Harry Marlar and his little sister, Ida.

Darkness seemed to surround Tina as she realized what she had done. Ida's card would likely never be found if it stayed in that vent. Tina tried one final time to grasp Ida's card. She was so determined that she actually moved Ida's card up to the vent grate, but when the card touched the metal, it slipped away from her and ended up even further down the vent. "Noooooo!" she howled. "That card is Ida's only chance!"

Tina knew what was coming, and within moments she felt the suction begin pulling at her back. Her assignment was over. She was being removed for tampering with the mortal world, and she knew she deserved it.

# CHAPTER THIRTY-FOUR

Tina was immediately summoned before the council. Brother Dalton was kind but firm as he said, "Sorry, Tina, but you are being permanently banned from any further assignments in the mortal world."

"I understand," Tina said. "Are other spirits able to move things so easily?"

"Actually, no," Brother Dalton said. "If anything, you're almost too good at this assignment. Your family needs to develop faith, and your ability to tinker with the mortal world is too strong to risk destroying that faith. Please return to your home in Paradise and await your reassignment." He then smiled. "I'm just glad you're on our side, because you would make one heck of a poltergeist."

Tina smiled faintly, but thoughts of Ida filled her mind. She knew Ida now had no chance to ever make it to Paradise before the Millennium. Things looked pretty bleak for her Inca ancestors, too, and it was all her fault.

Tina went home and sat quietly on the mansion's porch. Despite being surrounded by beauty, she felt all was lost. The council had been more than fair with her, and she would've made the same decision if she was in their position.

Tina thought of her parents and grew even more despondent. She had little hope Carmen would join the church without Frank's permission. She would likely have to divorce him to do so, and that was the last thing Tina wanted. It hurt Tina to think she wouldn't be allowed to see her family again until they entered the Spirit World themselves. Where would her parents end up? Frank seemed certain to live forever in a lower kingdom.

As these thoughts rolled through her head, an idea struck Tina so forcefully that she knew it must be inspired. "No, the council would never agree to it," she told herself, but if the idea was so unique they just might give it a try!

Tina soon stood again in the center of the council chambers. The council had a busy schedule, and Tina had patiently waited for a turn to share her plan. She had asked her grandma to be there with her, and Lucille now stood at the back of the room.

"Hello again, Brother Dalton," Tina said humbly.

Brother Dalton looked concerned to see her again so soon.

"Please be patient, Tina," he said. "We're working on your reassignment."

"Thank you," Tina said, "but that isn't why I am here. I have an unusual request. I would never have bothered you with it, but I feel my father is doomed unless we take a drastic measure."

The council was silent, so Tina added, "Grandma Lucille was a wonderful family historian and temple worker while on earth. Without her, thousands of our family members would still be trapped in Spirit Prison. So this request could be looked upon as a reward for her diligent service."

Brother Dalton nodded. "Yes, she has done everything asked of her. What is your request?"

"I propose that Grandma Lucille be allowed to write a story about what has happened to me since my family moved to Utah. Maybe it would change my father's heart. I could write it myself, but Grandma would do a much better job."

Brother Dalton was thoughtful. "What would you do with this story once it was written?"

Tina grew a bit bolder. "We could somehow transport it to the mortal world and let someone find it who can get it into my family's hands."

Tina glanced back at Lucille, who seemed to be in favor of the idea. The council paused to discuss the measure, but finally the word came back.

"There have been times when genealogical records that were created here in the Spirit World were placed into the hands of mortals," Brother Dalton said. "So your idea isn't unprecedented, but the council feels the idea is just too unorthodox for this situation. Keep thinking, though. You'll come up with something."

Tina lowered her head, knowing her idea would have worked, but she knew she was in no position to argue with the council. She began to leave the council chambers when Lucille stepped beside her and said, "Pardon me for being direct, but I think the council's decision is shortsighted."

Brother Dalton wasn't offended. He'd known Lucille long enough to know there must be a reason for her strong feelings.

"Why do you think this would work?" he asked.

Lucille turned to Tina. "Don't yield the floor to anyone until I get back."

Without responding to Brother Dalton, Lucille zoomed out of the room, and within a short time, a large ruckus could be heard outside the council chambers. Brother Dalton said to Tina, "Please open the door and see what is going on."

Tina cracked open the door and saw thousands of spirits descending outside. Lucille was among them, and she led one radiant spirit to Tina's side.

"These thousands of spirits are all descendants of this man, Benjamin Franklin Marlar," Lucille said. "They all support Tina's idea to have a book written. I personally think it is Frank's last chance. Also, once Josh graduates from Kansas State, he and Kim will be moving away. Those Kansas records will be left untouched again for several years. Kim has hardly begun to uncover what is there."

Tina watched the faces of the council members. She could see they were wavering a little. Lucille continued, "Think of all these souls who are now ready to move to Paradise. They just need someone to do their temple work. If you reject this idea, the work on both sides of the veil for this group will be delayed until the Millennium. What a shame that would be for Carmen's ancestors, not to mention Ida Marlar. And if it fails, so what? At least we tried."

A smile crossed Brother Dalton's face as he looked at the other council members. "Brethren, I believe Sister Marlar has made a good point. I propose we allow Lucille Marlar to write a short book that shares what has transpired in her son Frank's family during the past year. This book will be placed where someone can get it published. Is the council in agreement?"

Each member of the council raised his hand, and a shout erupted from the thousands of Marlar family members surrounding the building. Brother Dalton raised his hand for silence.

"I know of a man in Provo named Guy Calvert," he said. "He's a good man, and he has the ability to get it published. Plus, he will soon be called to serve a mission in Kansas and could get the book into Kim's hands." Brother Dalton then added with a twinkle in his eye, "Of course, he doesn't know it yet."

Brother Dalton looked at Lucille. "Another of my beautiful great-great-granddaughters is getting married in the Provo Temple next Saturday," he said. "I'll be attending the sealing and I could drop the book off at Guy's office on the way. He'll find it Monday morning, and we'll see how things go from there. I would like to read it first, though. Sister Marlar, could you have the manuscript ready by then?"

Tina started to protest, feeling that was not enough time, but Lucille said, "It will be ready."

"Wonderful," Brother Dalton said. "One word of caution. I'm sure your family members on earth would love a flowery description of the Spirit World, but please keep that to a minimum. The key is helping Frank and Carmen see the truth, rather than give them a tour of the Spirit World."

"I'll do my best," Lucille said. "We all realize this might be Frank's last chance."

Brother Dalton then looked at Tina and smiled. "Why don't you add your own page or two at the end? Let your family know you love them."

Brother Dalton stood, and the other council members joined him. "I believe we are done here," he said. "We need to let Sister Marlar get to work!"

The large crowd let out another joyful cheer. If all went well, many more of their extended family would soon be crossing over into Paradise.

As Lucille left the building, Ida was standing at the front of the crowd. She said, "Don't forget to write about me!"

"You'll be in there," Lucille said. "This is going to work!"

# A Message from Tina

─────── ❧ ───────

I am adding these final words at Brother Dalton's invitation. Grandma Lucille went straight from the meeting to our mansion, where she has been writing non-stop. She finished not long ago, and when I have finished this short addition, we are taking the manuscript to Brother Dalton so he can read it before departing for Provo.

I have read through the book, and I think Grandma has covered everything, so I just want to tell my family that I appreciate them even more now than I ever did while I lived on earth. My only regret is that I can no longer visit you. But during the year or so that I watched you after my death, I grew to love you more each day.

Kim, I am so proud of you. You have shown great courage in accepting the gospel. I did my best to help you, like fighting with Ruby during that first missionary discussion, but for the most part you just followed your heart and succeeded on your own. You and Josh have a special relationship, and I'm certain you will raise a righteous family.

As you might have guessed, my only request is that you go find Ida's records in that courthouse vent. That will erase one of my many blunders. Ida is so excited that she might finally get to come to Paradise. It's a dream she's been chasing for so long. Please make that happen as soon as possible.

Mom, I know you gained a good understanding of the gospel when you listened to Kim's missionary discussions. I also know you felt good at Kim's baptism and later in the temple visitors center during Kim's wedding. Please take the next step and join the LDS Church yourself. Thank you for all you have done for me.

I want to apologize for sending that Book of Mormon flying at you, but I was desperate for you to accept the gospel. Your ancestors are amazing people, and if you are able to find their records, I will return among them and lead them into Paradise. I beg you to make that one of your top priorities.

Dad, all I ask is that you do the right thing. You still have time to repent and take Mom to the temple. I forgive you for the past, and I hope the future is much brighter. My greatest hope is that when the time comes for you to come to the Spirit World, I will be able to greet you with a big hug here in Paradise. I will be greatly disappointed if I have to go find you in Spirit Prison, because that will mean you didn't change. Then your chances of ever making it to Paradise and eventually the Celestial Kingdom will be small. You know the gospel is true. Turn again to the Savior and make us an eternal family.

I have two final favors. Please let Roger Harmer know I don't hold any bad feelings toward him for what happened the night I died, and also contact Mrs. Hunter, who was driving the car that hit me. Accidents happen, and let them both know I'm doing fine.

Grandma Lucille has just come into my room. She said we need to take the manuscript to Brother Dalton now, so I must close. There are so many beautiful things about the Spirit World that Grandma and I weren't allowed to share, but I hope we can all live together someday here in Paradise. My mansion is now under construction, and it will have plenty of extra rooms. I'm hoping you will each stay with me until your own mansions are built.

I love you!

Your daughter and sister,

Tina

Dear gentlemen,

My name is Kim Brown, the sister of Tina Marlar. I have become friends with Elder Guy Calvert, a missionary for the LDS Church here in Kansas. He seemed very interested to share with me a copy of the galley proofs for the book *Chasing Paradise*. He claims to have found the book in his office a few months ago, even before he got his mission call.

I read the first few chapters of the book, and at first I became a bit angry. I sensed that someone had heard about my sister's death, turned it into a ghost story, and was now hoping to profit from it. But as I continued to read about incidents in my life that no one on earth could know, I knew this book had to be true. I finished reading it and could hardly contain my excitement, especially for Tina. She is doing so well, and in retrospect I have felt her presence many times.

However, I hesitated to share the book with my parents. As Grandma Lucille describes, my father has always been critical of the LDS Church. But now I understood why, and I knew if there was any chance of touching his heart, this book was it. So I went to a nearby copy center, copied the book, mailed it off, and called Mom to tell her she needed to read it as soon as it arrived.

Mom received the manuscript the next day. She had already finished reading it before Dad got home from work, and she called me to say she also felt it was true. That night she asked Dad to read it. He did so, but as expected, he didn't react too well. He only read for a few minutes before he told Mom it was trash. He asked who wrote it, and Mom explained to him how I had received it. Dad went nuts. He was convinced Elder Calvert had written the book as a way to get Mom to join the Church. Mom told him he was acting ridiculous, and that she had never even met Elder Calvert. They got into a horrible argument that lasted past midnight. Dad ended up sleeping on the couch.

Dad finally went into their bedroom at 3 a.m. and told her, "There's only one way to solve this. Get dressed. We're going to talk to Elder Calvert."

Within twenty minutes they were on the freeway heading south, arriving the next morning at my apartment in Manhattan, Kansas. Josh had just gone to school, and I was on my way to work. I was stunned to see them, and Dad hardly said "hello" before going straight to our bedroom to get some sleep. I called my employer to tell them I had a family emergency, then Mom and I spent the rest of the morning discussing the book.

When Dad finally woke up around noon, he faced two very determined women. He told us his conspiracy theory about Elder Calvert, but we just smiled kindly at his crazy ideas. This put him in an even grumpier mood, and he demanded to see Elder Calvert. Mom and I argued that he should read the whole story first, but he was sure that some direct questions to Elder Calvert would easily show that the book was a fake.

I called Elder and Sister Calvert, and I caught them during a lunch break at their apartment. They agreed to come over immediately. Meanwhile, Dad paced around, trying to keep his anger in check. I was afraid Elder Calvert was going to get a full blast of Dad's temper.

When we heard a car pull into the parking lot, Mom and I both rushed toward the door, but Dad beat us to it. He threw the door open and saw an elderly couple coming to our door. Dad shouted, "Are you the Calverts?" They nodded nervously.

"Get in here," he said. "You've got some explaining to do."

I rushed forward and stood between Dad and the Calverts as they slipped into the apartment. Mom motioned for them to take a seat on the couch, and I sat on the floor in front of them, half-afraid Dad might lunge at them. I had seen him at his worst, but I'd never seen him this worked up.

Dad stood in front of the Calverts and asked, "How did you find out so much about me for your book? How did you know I grew up as a Mormon?"

Elder Calvert just shrugged. "I didn't know anything about you until I read the book."

"Then how did you know about my Air Force transfers around the world?" Dad asked.

Elder Calvert shrugged again. "Like I said, I'd never even heard of you until I read the book."

"Then how did you write this thing?" Dad asked in disbelief. "Just some lucky guesses?"

Elder Calvert just stared back at him and said, "Do you really think I wrote that book? I'm no writer! Look at these hands!" He showed Dad his gnarled fingers. "I can hammer nails all day, but I could never write a book!"

Then Dad pointed at Sister Calvert. "So she typed it up as you told it to her?"

"She did type it, but from the manuscript I found on my desk," Elder Calvert said calmly, looking Dad straight in the eye. "She didn't change a word. This book is true, as sure as I'm sitting here."

Elder Calvert spoke with such conviction that although Dad still didn't believe him, his anger was slipping away. Dad stepped back and leaned against the wall, and to my surprise, Mom now stepped forward.

"I know the book is true," she said. "I can feel it in my heart. I believe Tina has accepted the truth, and I've seen how the Church has helped Kim become a wonderful person. Can you teach me more about it and help me get baptized?"

Dad groaned in defeat and slumped tiredly to the floor.

"We'll gladly teach you the lessons," Sister Calvert said. "Would that be all right, Mr. Marlar?"

Dad was so dismayed he just waved his hand.

"Whatever," he said. "She's a grown woman. But I'm not staying here. Carmen, I'll go get us a hotel room. I've already heard this Mormon junk before."

Dad got up to leave, but Elder Calvert stopped him. "Before you go, I have a gift for you," he said.

"Haven't you given me enough already?" Dad asked him in despair.

Dad tried to step past him, but Elder Calvert opened a briefcase and pulled out a stack of shimmering white paper.

"This is the original manuscript that I found on my desk in Utah," Elder Calvert said. "I'm sure Tina would want for you to have it."

Dad was taken by surprise, but he grabbed the pages. He went straight to the car, and we watched out the window as he drove away. After a few moments, the Calverts offered to teach Mom a discussion while we waited for Dad to return.

Dad did eventually return a few hours later, worn out and humbled. He told us a marvelous experience. I had him write it down for me for our family history, and here's what he wrote:

*After leaving Kim's apartment, I spotted a Best Western hotel and pulled into the parking lot. I quickly got a room, then carried the manuscript there. I put it on the bed and just stared at it. It seemed impossible. Did my daughter still live?*

*I thought back to my conversation with the Calverts. They had seemed completely sincere. What if this whole story were true? I pulled the hair on my head in agony, because if it were true, that would mean I had been wrong all of these years.*

*It felt like my heart was exploding. I fell face-first onto the carpet. Then from somewhere out of my past these words escaped from my mouth, "Heavenly Father, please help me."*

*I couldn't believe what I had said, but it felt so right. So I continued on with that prayer, pouring out my soul to him. I continued on for several minutes, telling him I felt worthless, but that I might be willing to change. Then I lay quietly, waiting for an answer. Nothing came.*

*Nothing at all. But I did feel calmer. I decided to try reading the manuscript.*

*This original version obviously didn't have Mr. Calvert's letter at the front and all the copyright stuff that the galley proofs had. It had a simple cover page that read, "Chasing Paradise."*

*Then the story began, "The elegant two-story building once again caught Tina Marlar's eye . . ."*

*I stared at that handwriting in disbelief. It was my mother's— exactly as if she were writing out a note excusing me from school!*

*It was a shock to my system to see her handwriting, but I finally started reading. I read again about parking in front of my old house in Nephi, which is where I had stopped reading the typed version of the manuscript. Then came an even greater shock. My mother had met Tina on the other side! Could it be true?*

*I felt a burning in my chest as I read through the rest of the book. I was reconnecting with my daughter and parents, and I was overjoyed with the experiences they were having on the other side of the veil. I even liked the many parts where Mom painted me as a scoundrel, because I am a scoundrel.*

*I had to pause and wipe away my tears when I read that my younger sister Evelyn had apparently died. I put the manuscript down and placed a call to our family home in Nephi. After all these years I still remembered the phone number.*

*A woman answered the phone. I asked if she was Teresa. She said yes, and I asked if her sister Evelyn had died. After a pause, Teresa asked, "Frank, is this you?"*

*I quietly said, "Yes."*

*"Oh Frank, I've been waiting so long for this call. Yes, Evelyn has passed away."*

*We spoke for several minutes, and it was wonderful to hear her voice. I promised to call back, and I said I would even visit her soon.*

*I was now emotionally drained, but I continued reading, becoming more convinced with each page that the story was true.*

*The final piece of the puzzle came when I read that Tina had met my dog Zipper. He had been my best friend and hiking companion in the hills above Nephi when I was a young boy. There's no way anyone on earth would have known that. I'm glad Zipper is happily living with my parents in Paradise. Finally, as I read Tina's words to me on the last page, the tears flowed freely. I knew I wouldn't be a scoundrel for much longer.*

*It had taken me all afternoon to read the book, and with those heavy hotel curtains I hadn't realized it had already gotten dark. With a sense of purpose I hadn't felt in a long time, I got back in the car and returned to Kim's apartment.*

*Josh met me at the door. "Frank, I understand there was some trouble here this morning," he said gently but firmly. "If you're going to come in, all I ask is that you keep your temper."*

*I told him that wouldn't be a problem. I followed him in and found Carmen and Kim cautiously watching the entryway.*

*"Hello," I said happily. "Anything new?"*

*They looked at each other, wondering what I was up to. Finally Carmen said, "The Calverts stayed several hours and taught me the first three discussions. Frank, I'm going to be baptized."*

*I stepped forward, and she nervously backed away from me. But then I stopped and held out my arms.*

*"Come here, Carmen," I said. "That is wonderful news. I'm happy for you."*

*Her jaw dropped, but she fell into my arms. Then Kim came over and embraced us, and Josh even patted my shoulder a little. After a minute, we all took a seat and I told them what I had experienced. I hardly believed it myself, but they were thrilled at my change of heart.*

A miracle had truly happened. Mom and Dad stayed in town for several days, and Mom just couldn't get enough of the gospel. She was eager to join the Church, and the Calverts taught her the rest of the discussions. On the following Sunday, Mom was baptized by Elder Calvert and confirmed a member of the Church by Josh.

My parents are now back in Nebraska, but Dad is suddenly dissatisfied with Air Force life. He plans on retiring soon, and they'll be moving closer to us. Another reason they'll be moving here is that after Mom's baptism Dad spent several minutes talking with our bishop. Bishop Maxwell told Dad he had also served in the Air Force, and they immediately hit it off.

The bishop seemed to sense that Dad's rough exterior merely covered the spirit of a man who had been unexpectedly humbled. Dad sheepishly explained to the bishop that he had asked for his name to be removed from the records of the Church when he first joined the Air Force, but that he was now ready to rejoin. Dad knows his journey back won't be easy, but he feels Bishop Maxwell is the man to help him.

Dad has suffered much anguish over his past behavior, and the hardest thing of all might be forgiving himself, because he feels Tina might still be alive if he had stayed true to the faith. But I told him that all he can do now is move forward. It might be a while before he can be re-baptized, and it will take him a year after that to be able to attend the temple. But he wants his family to be together forever. Hopefully Tina can patiently wait for Dad to get back on track.

Mom says it seems he has changed overnight, but Dad says that really isn't true. He says he has just returned to his roots, so to speak. At age 16 he knew the church was true, and now at age 44 he again knows it is true. Like in the Vision of the Tree of Life in the Book of Mormon, the mists of darkness caused Dad to get disoriented for a while, but now the air around him has cleared and he has found the Iron Rod again.

Also, I thought you might want to know I've been busy doing research on Ida Marlar. After reading the book, I returned to the Osborne County courthouse and with Dave's help I used a flashlight to spot the cards containing Harry's and Ida's death records down in the vent. Dave was very kind to remove the grate and retrieve the cards. He couldn't believe I knew they were down there. I also returned to Ida's tombstone. I took a rubbing of the stone, and almost miraculously "Ida Marlar" appeared on the paper.

I'll be traveling to Omaha and staying with my parents this

coming week. I'm going to the Winter Quarters Temple to do Ida's temple work. So there will soon be another vacancy in that Marlar apartment complex in Spirit Prison. Ida has waited long enough.

And finally, Mom has made contact with her parents after more than twenty years. In two months we are all going to fly down there to meet them and hopefully do a little missionary work. Dad will be arriving in Peru twenty-five years later than he should have, but maybe he can still do some good. Mom wants to find out the names of as many deceased family members as possible so we can do the temple work for them.

She has contacted a genealogical society in Peru that has a written history of the Inca leader Nimhi, and Josh is prepared to hike all through the jungle to find my extended family. We'll also do the best we can to find the records of the rest of Nimhi's descendants and do their temple work. We hope to keep Tina busy moving people into Paradise.

Anyway, I just wanted those of you who are publishing the book to know that even if you don't believe it, I know the story is true. If you feel it is appropriate, I would hope there is still time before the book goes to press to slip this letter in at the end. Readers might want to know that Tina's efforts in our behalf did pay off. I will always be grateful to her. She never gave up on our family, and we can't wait to be with her again.

Sincerely,

Kim Marlar Brown

# About the Author

Chad Daybell has worked in the publishing business for the past two decades and has written more than 25 books.

*Chasing Paradise* serves as a bridge between Chad's first novels, known as *The Emma Trilogy*, and the *Standing in Holy Places* series, where Josh and Kim Brown play key roles.

Chad is also known for his bestselling *Times of Turmoil* series, as well as his non-fiction books for youth, including *The Aaronic Priesthood* and *Baptism*. He and his wife Tammy also created the *Tiny Talks* series for Primary children.

He recently released his autobiography titled *Living on the Edge of Heaven*. In the book he shares many personal spiritual experiences that have shaped his life, and why he has felt inspired to write these books.

He is the president of Spring Creek Book Company. Visit **www.springcreekbooks.com** to see the company's lineup of titles.

Learn about Chad at his personal website **www.cdaybell.com** where he regularly gives updates about his books and experiences.

# GLIMPSES THROUGH THE VEIL

If you enjoyed *Chasing Paradise*, don't miss Chad Daybell's video series *Glimpses Through the Veil*, which tells of his two near-death experiences and gives the full story behind why he writes his novels.

Each episode is approximately 40 minutes long. The entire series is available for $30 through the video subscription service **www.Vimeo.com**.

Chad joins host Mike James to discuss a variety of topics regarding the other side of the veil in 10 fascinating episodes.

*1. A Tour Through the Spirit World*
*2. What Spirits Do After They Die*
*3. The Reality of Ghosts*
*4. The Role of Angels on Earth and in Heaven*
*5. What Children See When They Cross Over*
*6. We Plan Our Own Earthly Journey Before Birth*
*7. Our Life Review and Earning Our Place in Heaven*
*8. Our Deceased Relatives Are Eager to Assist Us*
*9. Messages from Prominent People on the Other Side*
*10. Angelic Warnings About America's Future*

In the series, Chad recounts his journeys to the other side of the veil in greater detail than ever before and shares the near-death experiences of other people. He and Mike also discuss several movies and films about the Spirit World.

Go to **Vimeo.com** and type in "Glimpses Through the Veil." Then hit the subscribe button, and you will have the entire series at your fingertips, whether on your computer, phone or tablet.